Stones
in the
Glade

ISBN: 978-1-959883-57-9
Library of Congress Control Number on file.

Cover design by Becca Fleming.
Edited by Kumari Pacheco.

Published by:
Crossed Crow Books, LLC
6934 N Glenwood Ave, Suite C
Chicago, IL 60626
www.crossedcrowbooks.com

Printed in the United States of America.
IBI

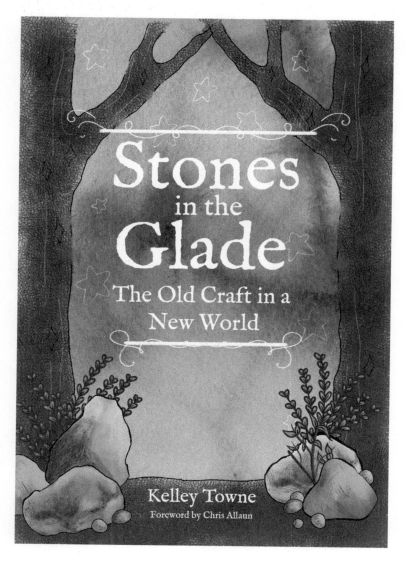

Stones
in the
Glade
The Old Craft in a
New World

Kelley Towne

Foreword by Chris Allaun

Chicago, IL

*To my family—thank you for being there in my corner and
supporting me in all my ventures, including this one.
You are a big reason for my successes in life.
To my ancestors—thank you for
watching over and guiding me.*

*To my brothers and sisters in the Craft—thank
you for being a reliable support system and a web
of mutual learning and growth. You are not
only my best friends but my second family.*

*To numerous others who have supported me over the
years—thank you all for being there. It means so much,
and your being there has been highly encouraging.*

TABLE OF CONTENTS

FOREWORD

I like to think I've been a Witch my whole life. When I was a child, I saw spirits and talked to ghosts. I knew the spirits that lived under my front porch and in the closet of my room. There was also a shadow that lived in our hallway. My little brother said that when I moved out of the house the shadow was sad that I had left. We lived out in the country near a small town just outside of Houston, and my brothers and I spent many days in the fields and the woods behind our home. The spirits of nature were all around me. It seems strange to admit this now, but growing up like I did I was so used to the spirits being around that I started to take them for granted.

Then, when I was seventeen, I found my first book on witchcraft. I studied every page and tried to practice what I could, but our religious household never would have allowed me to call myself a Witch. In fact, any gifts we did talk about growing up were said to have come from Jesus! I kept reading that book, taking from it those things that I found useful, but still the book left me feeling a bit unfulfilled. There was something missing that I desperately craved from magick.

As the years passed, I naturally found many other magick and witchcraft books and continued to learn what I could from them. I remember thinking there had to be more to magick than what was being sold at the local bookstores. I had a longing for deeper magick, but that longing would be unfulfilled for many years. Nevertheless, I continued to scour through the available books for a morsel of magick that was fulfilling.

I had a deep knowing in my gut that there was more to magick. I just needed to find it.

Skip ahead another decade, when I was 27 years old I was initiated into a Traditional Witchcraft group. I was thrilled to have the magical training that you could not find in books at the time. I learned to develop my psychic skills and go deeper into trance work and journey into the worlds of the spirits and gods. The thing about Traditional Witchcraft is that it's mostly intuition. When I would have a question about a technique my teacher would say, "What does it feel like?" or "What does your intuition say?" These are very good questions to ask a student but when you are learning to listen and trust your intuition you can become lost or even worse, self-deluded, if you do not have the proper skills and discernment for this type of witchcraft. As much as I had grown magically in those ten years, I couldn't help but feel like I was missing something.

In magick, sometimes we have this gnawing at our gut that is telling us something isn't quite right. It almost feels like our cauldrons are half full and we are waiting for a teacher, an ancestor, or, gods to help us fill it up the rest of the way. Don't get me wrong, I'm a tried-and-true Trad Crafter, but as I was learning, I felt like what I was looking for was slightly out of reach. Yes, one could say that the student wasn't ready. I think sometimes that's a cop out. When a student knows they are looking for a deeper connection it's up to the teacher to guide and train the student to a more fulfilling path.

That brings me to this book, *Stones in the Glade*. Kelley Towne is giving the seeker everything they need to start or continue their magical journey. What I like most about this book is that she allows the student to go deeper into both structured and intuitive witchcraft without gatekeeping or thinking they are not ready. Kelley trusts that the reader is able to make sound decisions for themselves, which empowers them to take that journey down the long and crooked road of Witchery.

This book doesn't shy away from teaching about the different psychic skills one needs to be a Witch, nor does it shy away from talking about the spirits needed to work powerful magick. I always felt that it was an odd thing when other books try to tell a student of witchcraft when they are and are not ready for certain types of magick. Want to hear a secret? If the spirits have guided you to this book then you are ready. Don't let anyone gatekeep you into thinking they know better. The Witch that knows better is you!

Kelley Towne teaches us in this book that there is magical power in dreams, familiar spirits, and the green world. I must admit, I am a little jealous of you as the reader!. You are embarking on an incredible journey into witchcraft that those of us from a different generation were not taught in books. In those days authors were afraid we would hurt ourselves. Truth be told, if you come to magick and witchcraft with an open heart and the mindset of "power with" and not "power over" then you will be fine as you learn to conjure familiar spirits and travel the astral realm with lucid dreaming. Kelley allows us to take responsibility for our own magick as well as our own development.

As you read and practice the workings in each of these chapters, know that you are tapping into an old and primal power—the Witch Ancestors—the Witches who have come before you and who have already gone through a similar journey on the crooked road. Connect to them. Listen to them. They are saying to take another step on the path of Witchcraft. Join us in the timeless art of Witchery, won't you? We are waiting for you.

– Chris Allaun
Author of *The Black Book of Johnathan Knotbristle*
July 2023

PREFACE

Perhaps it is appropriate to explain in brief how I—the author of this book—came onto my path as a Witch. I can attest from experience that being a practitioner is not easy, even if you are born for it. There is a lot of soul-searching involved; many personal deaths and rebirths occur in order to usher in those new beginnings that really change your views on not just the Craft but the world. I felt the pull to mysticism and magic when I was about eight years old. It was not until I was twelve that I began to study Wicca more seriously. Looking back, this was like a baby step for me. At seventeen, after contemplating the flaws I found within organized religion as a whole, I had an epiphany that led me into deeper things. It helped me move past the confines of religion and develop my own path based on whatever I could learn from traditional, pre-Gardnerian practices.

This is where my inner fire for the Old Craft was officially sparked, and it wasn't until around this time that I also realized said fire runs in my family. Intuitive and psychic gifts emerged in my mother's bloodline, but I am the very first in my family to call myself a Witch. I have my own gifts, my mother has hers, her mother had a few, but it was her mother before her who practiced things very similar to what I do today with her Italian Catholic folk magic. Now as an adult, my gifts have grown stronger and more numerous; what began as dreaming true in my preteen years later blossomed into spirit flight and spirit contact.

When I got to college—as a young adult past the whole *love and light* phase—I realized that I had no desire to become part of a coven. This decision to not join a coven was very personal for me, and I'm willing to bet that aspect is the same for anyone about to embark on this path. Around this time, I got the idea to write this book, which became a six-year project. It was also during this period that I became more atheistic in my Craft and learned self-reliance as part of my personal development. For about two years or so, I did not even work with deities. However, when I got back on track with just that, I felt like things were coming together once again, because there is nothing like being attuned and connected with the Old Ones in all of their primal glory.

So, what makes a Witch, really? You can be born with the predisposition for it, you can have the spark, but do you have what it takes to turn that spark into a fire—to tend it, feed it, and control it so that it doesn't destroy everything in its path? If so, keep going.

CHAPTER ONE

THE DEVIL IN NEW ENGLAND

Before delving into the contents of this book, it is very important to have some understanding of the complex history of Witchcraft in the early colonial period—particularly the trials and famous legends found throughout much of New England. Witchcraft and magic were a part of daily life in Europe, both heavily believed in and feared. These beliefs were brought to the New World by colonists and further spread. The English dominated the northeast from the time Plymouth, Massachusetts was founded in the 1620s, and from then on, the surrounding areas were called New England.

Today, this region of the US is made up of Maine, New Hampshire, Vermont, Rhode Island, Connecticut, and of course, Massachusetts. With the founding of this new territory, laws were set to regulate everyone's behavior, and since there was no separation of church and state yet, quite a few had religious inspiration. One law, written as early as 1636,[1] dictated that anyone who made a compact with the Devil through means of Witchcraft would be sentenced to death. This was based on a royal charter of the Massachusetts Bay Colony from 1629, which was used as a basis for enforcing laws in the early

---

1 Johnson, Caleb. "Crime and Punishment in Plymouth Colony." Mayflower History.com, 2014, mayflowerhistory.com/crime.

colonial period.[2] This charter included other laws that gave the death sentence for crimes like murder, perjury, adultery, blasphemy, and more. Needless to say, Puritan Massachusetts had the harshest laws—and the harshest punishments for those who broke them.

Why was there such hostility toward Witches? After the death of Queen Elizabeth I in 1603,[3] the crown was set on the head of James I, bringing a new dynasty to power in England. Hailing from the House of Stuart, James I had already been Scotland's king from the time he was a baby, as well as the heir to England's throne; upon his coronation, the two kingdoms became one. Historians generally agree that James I was not a very good king. He was intolerant and particularly despised Catholics and Puritans. He is very well-known for introducing the King James version of the Bible and for his bizarre obsession with Witches, which started at a young age. He saw Witches as a threat not only to his rule, but to society. King James I even went as far as to accuse Witches for the execution of his mother, Mary Queen of Scots. Fun fact—famous playwright William Shakespeare was inspired by King James I and his fascination with Witches to compose his masterpiece *Macbeth*.

There was more leniency toward Witchcraft in England before King James I rose to power, given that in Scotland, under his rule, it was already considered a very serious crime. There was also a clear distinction of types: white Witches (who served as healers) and black Witches (who caused harm and discord). In England, that line became blurred due to King James I's general mistrust of Witches; thus, many people were accused and executed for Witchcraft in both lands. One notable example from Scotland was in 1591, when healer

---

2   Berkshire Law Library. "Witchcraft Law up to the Salem Witchcraft Trials of 1692." Mass.gov, 31 Oct. 2017, mass.gov/news/witchcraft-law-up-to-the-salem-witchcraft-trials-of-1692.

3   "Elizabeth I (R.1558-1603)." The Royal Family, 3 Aug. 2018, royal.uk/elizabeth-i.

Agnes Sampson was burnt at the stake. She was accused of raising a storm the year prior when King James I and his wife, Anne of Denmark, were returning from her home country. Coincidentally, the Copenhagen Witch trials were happening that same year, which only made King James's paranoia worse. This fanaticism and hatred toward Witches spread to the New World despite the Puritans leaving England for the purpose of religious freedom.

Out of all the New England colonies, there is no record of a Witch trial or execution in Rhode Island.[4] For the time, this state was very tolerant and progressive, open to those who were rejected by Puritan communities. This does not mean that Rhode Island was devoid of any peculiar events, as in 1892, the town of Exeter saw a vampire scare with the case of Mercy Brown. Her entire family was afflicted with tuberculosis, and her body in particular was exhumed—her heart removed and burnt because the townspeople believed she was a vampire. Their basis for this was that she had fresh blood in her veins despite having been dead for weeks.[5]

Maine, the northernmost part of New England, was a territory which teetered between belonging to the British and the French. Interestingly, it actually was a part of Massachusetts, a British colony, prior to 1820 despite having mostly French influence. That said, the Candlemas Massacre of 1692 may have directly influenced the air of fear and terror during the Salem trials, as it reinforced the idea of an *invisible enemy*. Yet, this enemy wasn't invisible. During the massacre, the town of York, Maine was viciously attacked by the French, who used the Native

---

4   Greco, Karen. "The Witches of Providence." *Providence Monthly*, 30 Sept. 2022, providenceonline.com/stories/the-witches-of-providence,99049#.

5   Tucker, Abigail. "The Great New England Vampire Panic." *Smithsonian Magazine*, Oct. 2012, smithsonianmag.com/history/the-great-new-england-vampire-panic-36482878/.

Americans to do their dirty work; many people were killed, some were taken hostage, and buildings were burnt down.[6]

There is a legend about the final resting place of Colonel Jonathan Buck, for whom Maine's Buck Cemetery is named. Colonel Buck served as a judge in Massachusetts, where he was involved in the trial of a woman accused of Witchcraft. She was sentenced to hang, but in the process, she put a curse on him—that she would one day dance on his grave. When Colonel Buck was laid to rest in 1795, a shape began to form on his tombstone, resembling a leg. People were mystified by this and sought to get rid of the mark. After scrubbing it to no avail, they tried sanding it. It went away for a while, only to return.

In reality, there are no Witchcraft trials on record for the state of Maine, and Colonel Buck himself was born well after the Witchcraft hysteria of the seventeenth century.[7] It is important to note, however, that while Maine did not have any Witchcraft trials, they still believed in Witches enough to create such stories.

In Connecticut, the Hartford Witch trials were a series of accusations and executions lasting close to twenty years; they're considered to be the very first *large-scale* Witch trials to occur in the colonies.[8] In 1647, Alse Young was accused of Witchcraft—though being in a position to inherit her late husband's land may have played a part in her accusation to begin with. She was hanged at the age of thirty-two, and decades later, her own daughter was accused of Witchcraft in Springfield, Massachusetts. Alse's daughter was spared because it was simply a case of

---

6 Landrigan, Leslie. "The Candlemas Massacre and the Salem Witch Trials." New England Historical Society, 1 Mar. 2017, newenglandhistoricalsociety.com/candlemas-massacre-salem-witch-trials/.

7 Rogak, Lisa. *Stones and Bones of New England.* Rowman & Littlefield, 2016.

8 Pagliuco, Chris. "Connecticut's Witch Trials." Wethersfield Historical Society, 2007, wethersfieldhistory.org/articles/connecticuts-witch-trials/.

slander, despite the odd coincidence that an influenza outbreak had happened that same year. The first known confessor to Witchcraft was Mary Johnson, a housemaid accused of theft in 1648 while working for a family in nearby Wethersfield. While being whipped by the minister for this misdeed, she slipped that she had been "familiar" with the Devil and had killed a child. Whether she said this under duress is uncertain. She was pregnant at the time of her trial; after giving birth, she was hanged in 1650.

In 1669, Katherine Harrison was accused of Witchcraft during the Hartford trials, particularly for ditching Sabbath, fortune-telling, and practicing black magic. She was also accused of appearing to people in an astral form whilst they slept. Katherine had made her way to the top in society, coming from England in 1651 to become a housemaid of a captain, marrying the town crier, and inheriting his money and property after he died. The latter of the so-called powers she used on people was key in sparing her life, as the magistrates disagreed that it was truly grounds to execute her. She and her family were banished from Connecticut and settled in New York in 1670, thus ending the Hartford trials. During this twenty-year period, thirty-seven people were accused and eleven were sent to the gallows.

In New Hampshire, there are a few records of people accused of Witchcraft. In Portsmouth, Jane Walford was tried for Witchcraft three times starting in 1656, but each time, she was acquitted. She was married to a very important official in town, which may have been a protective factor. The first time, Jane was slandered by another local woman; the woman was fined two pounds after Jane took her to court. Sometime later, another townswoman accused Jane of emerging from the woods, conjuring fire with her hands, and turning into a cat while leaving the scene. A local couple added that Jane often transformed into a yellow cat that followed them, which the husband tried to kill. The third time, a man claimed that Jane came to him at night and painfully pressed on his chest so that he could not breathe.[9] Later, one of Jane's daughters was accused of Witchcraft, simply based on the idea that it ran in families.

Eunice Cole, colloquially known as "Goody Cole," made the voyage to the New World from England with her husband in 1630. The couple was in debt; they made New Hampshire their home, and Eunice developed a negative reputation for starting arguments with her neighbors over livestock and property boundaries. The Coles were also accused of slander and stealing pigs—when apprehended, it is said that Eunice bit the constable. Eventually, people started blaming Eunice for the things going wrong in their lives, like the deaths of their children or bad health of their cows. She went on to be accused a total of three times for Witchcraft but was repeatedly let off due to unsubstantiated evidence. Accusations against Eunice specifically included owning a familiar that scratched her neighbor's windows and having a blue mark on her body, the latter of which was discovered whilst she was being whipped. In 1680, she died widowed and penniless.

The townspeople did not care enough to give her a proper burial, so the affair was nonchalant. The exact whereabouts of her grave are unknown. However, there's a rather bizarre legend surrounding her burial—apparently, Eunice's body was buried with a stake in her heart and a horseshoe hanging on top of it in order to keep her spirit from doing any more harm to Hampton's residents. It was not until 1938 that Hampton's residents exonerated her, believing her to be merely a disgruntled, unpleasant old woman rather than a genuine Witch. The Goody Cole Society was founded, and during a public ceremony, town residents got together and burnt copies of court documents smeared with soil from what was thought to be her

---

9 "Complaint of Susannah Trimmings, of Little Harbour, Pascataqua." Witchcraft in New Hampshire - 1656, 18 Apr. 1656, n6jv.com/tena/witch.htm. This source is from an archive and historical document detailing Jane Walford's trial and the accusations leveled against her.

resting place. These were contained in an urn, which is now housed in the Tuck Museum. In 1963, a memorial stone was dedicated to Goody Cole in Hampton.[10]

Perhaps the most infamous and numerous Witch trials were those in Massachusetts. Charlestown's Margaret Jones, a midwife who practiced medicine, was the first to be accused and executed in 1648. Midwifery was a controversial profession because it meant that, in performing their duties, these women were a bridge between life and death. They also often had an intimate knowledge of medicinal plants that most physicians could only dream about—especially given that the latter frequently put leeches on patients, advised the ingestion of mercury, and practiced bloodletting. Margaret Jones had a reputation for predicting things that would come to pass, and for this and other reasons, she was imprisoned. John Winthrop, the governor of the colony and a prominent lawyer, documented Margaret closely, even watching her for a full day to see if an imp would come to her cell. Imps were seen as familiars to Witches, so this would have been considered damning evidence. Unsurprisingly, John claimed he saw one, and with so much evidence leveled against her, Margaret was sentenced to death.

Dorchester's Alice Lake, a mother of five, had a baby that died and saw visions of it often. To the Puritans, this didn't make Alice a grieving mother, but a Witch who was visited by the Devil in the form of her baby. She was given the chance to recant her story but instead mustered up an admission that the Devil was drawn to her due to premarital sex she had in her youth. This did not help her case, and she was hanged in 1648. In 1656 Springfield, Mary Parsons had a feud with Sarah Bridgman, her neighbor. While Mary was known for being outspoken, Sarah started accusing her of harming livestock, injuring people, and causing fits. Sarah faced slander charges with the court being in favor of Mary, but this relief was short-lived.

---

10 "Eunice 'Goody' Cole." Hampton Historical Society, 2011, hamptonhistorical-society.org/gcole.htm.

Sarah's daughter died suddenly in 1674, causing the accusations against Mary to continue. Despite being acquitted of Witchcraft charges, she was ostracized for the rest of her life.

Around 1650, Elizabeth Kendall of Cambridge was executed after being accused and convicted of bewitching a neighbor's daughter. She was a woman of modest standing, though said to be married to a younger man—quite scandalous for the time. In Boston that same year, Ann Hibbins was hanged for charges of Witchcraft. An incident where local carpenters overcharged her for work she'd needed done was enough to get her excommunicated, and this made her an easy target. Ann Hibbins was one inspiration for Nathaniel Hawthorn's classic masterpiece, *The Scarlet Letter*. In 1688, Irishwoman Ann Glover was accused in Boston on the basis that she was "speaking the devil's tongue," when in reality, Gaelic was her first language, and she did not know the Lord's Prayer in English. She was accused of praying to other gods and carrying dolls around—which may have been Catholic icons—and sentenced to hang.[11]

One fascinating case is that of the Groton Witch, also known as Elizabeth Knapp,[12] which was more so a case of possession. Sixteen-year-old Elizabeth was documented for strange behaviors between 1671 and 1672, while working as a servant in Reverend Samuel Willard's household. During this time, Reverend Willard sent letters about his observations to Cotton Mather, a prominent Puritan minister who was regarded as a great intellectual in the Massachusetts Bay Colony. Shortly after starting work in the Willard household, Elizabeth began to experience fits—laughing or screaming at random—as well as strange bodily pains that seared like fire. In particular, Elizabeth claimed that she was being strangled, in addition to having leg and breast pain. During the fits, her thrashing was so strong that four people could barely restrain her.

---

11 Muise, Peter. *Witches and Warlocks of Massachusetts Legends, Victims, and Sinister Spellcasters.* Globe Pequot, 2021.

12 Ibid.

Samuel Willard was an unorthodox reverend for his time, in that he called a physician for Elizabeth rather than relying on faith. When Elizabeth finally became lucid, she disclosed that the Devil had come to her for three years in various guises with the goal of making her sign his Black Book in exchange for painless labor, eternal youth, wealth, and other earthly pleasures. She also said that the Devil tried to coerce her into committing suicide or killing the Willard family. By December 1671, Elizabeth reached a catatonic state. When it ended, she claimed that she'd finally signed the Devil's book and let him into her bed. Her fits only grew worse, to the point where she would speak with a booming voice no one would expect out of a teenage girl. According to witness testimony, Elizabeth's throat swelled, and she would call Reverend Willard a rogue preacher and a liar.

By early 1672, Elizabeth claimed that the Devil had full control over her body and mind. Around this time, Reverend Willard's journal stopped containing entries about her. Did she ever live a normal, full life after this? Or did she die? Fortunately, Elizabeth Knapp not only survived the ordeal, but married Samuel Scripture, had children, and lived a relatively normal life until her passing in 1721.[13] Elizabeth's case was used as a model to explain the happenings in Salem Village by both Samuel Willard and Cotton Mather nearly twenty years later.

No question about it: the most famous Witch trials in the world were those in Salem. If you wish to learn more about the Salem Witch Trials, there are many books and articles written about them—but they will be explained in brief here. The trials began in March 1692, when Elizabeth Parris and Abigail Williams began to experience violent fits after experimenting with the fortune-telling of Tituba, the Parris family's Caribbean-Native American slave. Tituba often told stories about the indigenous practices of her homeland, which caught the interest of Elizabeth and Abigail's group of friends.

---

13 "Samuel Scripture (Abt1649-Abt1725) of Groton." Rjohara.net, rjohara.net/gen/scripture/.

Tituba was the very first to be accused in Salem after this was discovered. Hysteria spread around the village like wildfire, and by June, Bridget Bishop was the first to be executed.

In the months following, 150 men and women were imprisoned on Witchcraft accusations, and a total of nineteen townspeople were executed with one, Giles Corey, being pressed to death. His wife, Martha, also met her fate at the gallows. Three sisters—Rebecca Nurse, Mary Eastey, and Sarah Cloyce—were all accused. Rebecca and Mary were executed, but Sarah was spared. Interestingly, their mother, Joanna Towne, had been accused of Witchcraft in Topsfield around 1670 but had never been arrested nor tried due to unsubstantiated evidence. It is likely that these accusations came about due to property disputes with the prominent Putnam family.[14]

All of these cases had the following testimonies in common: that the accused owned familiar spirits, utilized poppets, left their bodies in spirit form to terrorize the village girls or other townsfolk, and caused people to have fits or become possessed. However, most of these executions were in vain or had selfish motives behind them. Not only did the Puritans of New England let their paranoia and fear rule their lives, but also their greed; if someone was to inherit property, they could easily point fingers and call that person a Witch to get them killed. As for the fits and hysteria, scientists and doctors have tried to debunk what really happened to the victims—everything from ergotism to seizures have been proposed as causes. Of course, it goes without saying that the fanatical Puritans had a very poor understanding of what real Witchcraft or magic was. Ironically, they brought apotropaic items with them to the New World, like Witch bottles. Today, many memorials and museums stand as a reminder of Salem's dark past—and to illustrate

---

14 The Atwell Family. "Sarah Towne of Salem, Massachusetts, Part 2: The Accusers and Accused." *Tree of Many Leaves*, 30 May 2019, treeofmanyleaves.com/treeofmanyleaves/2019/4/11/sarah-towne-of-salem-massachusetts-part-2-the-accusers-and-accused.

just how much and how far ignorance can take people in the wrong direction.

After the seventeenth century, there weren't as many Witch trials in New England, let alone the whole of the colonies, but people were still being tried and executed in Europe and other parts of the world. Today in New England, the overall attitude toward Witchcraft has changed—especially within Salem, now a safe haven for those with mystical leanings of all kinds. People are more open nowadays to getting divinations done on themselves, for novelty or entertainment if not for answering serious questions. Additionally, the Devil that the old Puritans knew is not the same one that some Witches recognize. Rather, he is a folk being who rules all wild places, including the untamed ones within us.

CHAPTER TWO

BEGINNINGS

The Witchcraft we'll be covering in this book is a stream of practice involving magic that is European in origin. Magic, in turn, is the manipulation of energy to obtain a desired result. For practitioners of Witchcraft, utilizing magic also depends on one's relationship with the natural world and all that resides within it. For many modern practitioners, it is both a religion and *not*; some today would argue that this ancient art is only a spiritual practice and a skill upon which one can improve over time. To others, especially in initiatory circles and established traditions, it is considered a religion with a core set of beliefs and practices that are handed down and taught. This spiritual path has gradually become more accepted with many twists and changes, but there is still some stigma attached to it along with numerous misconceptions. Even in this day and age, people still call Witches "devil worshippers" or "evil"— especially those stuck in their ignorant ways or who have an intense fear of Witchcraft altogether.

In reference to the title of this chapter, there are many things that make a Witch. A common question is whether a Witch is born or made through initiation, study, and practice. I think it's both. You do not come out of the womb knowing how to do rituals or with an uncanny knowledge of magical theory— you have to be taught that part and apply that knowledge to your practice. A Witch can learn of their gifts at a young age and have a family history of such gifts before they even discover who they truly are. It is no secret that children are known to be psychically gifted and receptive to things that most adults have long since shut themselves off to.

Certain gifts being inherited is not a new concept, but when it comes to practices that have been handed down, a centuries-long, pure, and unbroken line is almost impossible to find today—especially taking into account that many people prior to the twentieth century were illiterate and did not have access to an adequate education. Nothing could be written down; things passed by word of mouth tend to change over time or become lost due to not having been recorded anywhere or practiced continuously. In other cases, family traditions or practices even in the most mundane sense are modified or added to in order to fit the changing times. Even so, throughout the ages, a Witch was said to inherit their talents through a parent or by spiritual ancestry—the latter of which is gained by initiation into one of the many traditions of the Craft.

Another account of the origin of Witches is biblical, as it claims Witch-blood started with Cain, who killed his half-brother, Abel.[15] It is very important to note that "Witch-blood" does not refer to a literal bloodline, but rather the spiritual lineage from which Witches are said to descend. There are many different versions of this biblical story, but the common one says Cain killed his brother out of jealousy, because Abel was capable of yielding more crops than he. Cain's mother was Eve; her other son, Abel, was fathered by Adam. However, there is a lot of debate about who Cain's real father is.

In one account, Cain is actually the result of Eve lying with the serpent, a form which Lucifer took. Thus, in this version of events, Lucifer is likely Cain's real father. However, most people accept that Adam is Cain's real father. As Abel was killed, his blood soaked the ground, which enacted a curse not only on the land but on Cain himself. Cain was granted a distinctive mark

---

15 Genesis 4. *The Holy Bible: New International Version.* Zondervan, 1984.

that protected him from harm. On the flipside, God handed him a punishment in which he would wander the earth for all eternity, and that any land he attempted to farm would be sterile and unfit for life. Cain, however, managed to father his own lineage, building a city just east of Eden that his descendants happily expanded.[16] He was the ancestor of Tubal-Cain, the first blacksmith, as well as Lamech, who is said to have killed Cain, thus creating a full circle in his story's arc.

There is also the prevailing and intriguing origin of Witch-blood through the *Grigori,* otherwise known as "the Watchers." Detailed in the Book of Enoch, these were angels sent to Earth in order to oversee mankind's progress and development while interfering very little in their lives.[17] This all changed when they became attracted to the most beautiful of Earth's women and decided to mingle with them. The Watchers started teaching them forbidden skills like cosmetics, personal adornment, weapon crafting, and of course, sorcery and divination. In hindsight, the knowledge these earthly women gained from the Watchers could be a reason why, historically, they have been targeted in Witch trials and ostracized. Perhaps the predominantly male-oriented—organized religion did not want godly powers in the hands of women? A race of giants called the Nephilim were the offspring of these fallen angels and human women, said to be "men of renown." God was enraged to learn that the angels he'd dispatched to Earth disobeyed him, to the point where he sent the Great Flood to purge the world of sin. Most of Cain's descendants were also said to have been wiped out in this Flood, except for one, named Noah. The angel Uriel warned Noah about the oncoming flood, instructing him on how to escape this fate. Thus, the story of Noah loading his family and animal pairs onto his Ark comes into play.

Even older than Abrahamic lore and religion is the archetype of the being who can perform magic or shape destiny, shown in

16 Howard, Michael. Children of Cain. Three Hands Press, 2019.
17 Charles, R H. *The Book of Enoch.* Dover Publications, 2007.

various cultures throughout thousands of years. From deities to figures in legends, every recorded culture has had some idea about the manipulation of nature to achieve a desire, specifically through a symbiotic relationship with the natural world and the universe at large. Granted, most of these cultures did not call these figures "Witches," especially since the word "Witch" did not come about until the Anglo-Saxon period. Among the Greeks was the goddess Hecate, who ruled not only over Witchcraft but the crossroads. Within this culture, we also find figures like Circe, who, in the *Odyssey*, turned some of Odysseus's men into pigs. Her niece Medea, the wife of Jason, was gifted in the herbal arts with a specialty in poisons and used this to get revenge on her husband for his infidelity—with tragic consequences.

In ancient Rome, the moon goddess Diana was heavily associated with Witchcraft even up into the medieval and Renaissance eras of Italy, known as the "Queen of Faeries" who harbored the secrets of magic.[18] In Scandinavia, we see many figures possessing the power to change and weave fate—Freyja, the goddess of love, was a master at *seiðr*, a form of magic involving trances and communions with the gods that was primarily practiced by women. She also possessed the ability to fly between the realms, wearing a special falcon raiment. The Allfather, Odin, was also gifted in magic, having been taught its secrets by the Vanir as well as gained wisdom from being hung from Yggdrasil after sacrificing one of his eyes. The Völuspá, one of many poems in the Poetic Eddas, tells of how Odin consulted a seeress in order to learn about the way in which the world was created—and how it would end. Frigg, Odin's wife, ruled over prophecy and spent a lot of time spinning the fates of thousands, the caveat being that she could never tell someone their true fate as she wove it.

18 Leland, Charles G. *Aradia: Gospel of the Witches.* 1899.

Magic played a role in everyday life not just for the Norse people but for the Celts. In ancient Wales, we find goddesses like Cerridwyn, who could shapeshift into various animals and famously kept a cauldron. Arianrhod graced the night sky as the moon and stars, with her magical feats of shapeshifting described in the *Mabinogion*. As a main character in *Math the Son of Mathonwy*,[19] she slays her son—who takes the form of Lleu Llaw Gyffes—by adopting the form of Blodeuwedd, a goddess cursed to live eternity as an owl. The owl representing wisdom, feeds on her son's flesh, but he in turn becomes an eagle and is restored to life.[20] Ireland's mythical race, the Tuatha Dé Danann, embraced magic in their everyday lives; their matriarch, Danu, was heavily associated with faerie mounds and life on Earth as the Celts knew it. The war goddess Morrígan was associated with magic and revenge in ancient Ireland, her form of a crow flying over battlefields to pluck the flesh from the slain. Brigid ruled over various crafts like smithing, poetry, and of course, magic and prophecy. Later, we see magical figures in Arthurian tales, like Merlin and Morgan le Fay—the latter of whom is associated with Avalon and the sea.

In the enigmatic Basque country between Spain and France, there are legends of the *sorginak*, who were attendants to the goddess Mari and met weekly on Fridays.[21] This same term is used to describe what the English-speaking world would call "Witches." Going east to Russia, we find the hag Baba Yaga, who is said to live in a hut supported by bird's feet, representing that person on the fringes of society who may hinder or help whoever is seeking their aid.

---

19 "The Mabinogion: Math the Son of Mathonwy." Sacred-Texts.com, sacred-texts.com/neu/celt/mab/mab26.htm.

20 Graves, Robert, and Grevel Lindop. *The White Goddess: A Historical Grammar of Poetic Myth.* Farrar, Straus, and Giroux, 2013.

21 Whalen, R. "Sorginak and the Basque Witch Trials." Basque at the University of Illinois at Urbana-Champaign, 21 Feb. 2015, basqueuiuc.wordpress.com/2015/02/21/sorginak-and-the-basque-witch-trials/.

With countless tales from Europe alone, what about other parts of the world? Didn't they have figures who could work magic in their own ways? In the cradle of civilization, Mesopotamia, we find Lilith, described as Adam's first wife in the Abrahamic religions, who, unlike Eve, grew from the Earth itself rather than being taken from Adam's rib.[22] However, in Sumer and Babylonia, she is depicted as a demon who preys on babies and causes erotic dreams in men, as well as a powerful spirit of wind and storms.[23] She is also compared to goddesses like Inanna and Ereshkigal, specifically because of her betwixt and in-between nature. She can fly through the night and heavens but also has her roots in the great, dark below. A common trait she shares with Inanna is her association with love, sexuality, and sovereignty. On the other hand, Lilith and Ereshkigal share an affinity with darkness, death, and subterranean realms.

On a related note, there is an ongoing debate about who the Burney Relief depicts. This engraving—which dates to the nineteenth century BCE—depicts a winged, crowned female figure in terra cotta, her arms bent up while holding rod-and-rings. These were symbols of authority and respect in ancient Mesopotamia, and those depicted holding them are usually either kings or gods. The figure is also flanked by owls and lions on each side at her taloned feet. This artifact has been dubbed "Queen of the Night," a name that usually refers to Lilith, but it's thought to depict any one of these three entities: Lilith (who is able to fly between worlds, the screech owl serving as one of her associations), Innana (who, as the Queen of Heaven, travels similarly and was associated with sexuality and lust just as Lilith is), or Ereshkigal (the Queen of the Great Below, ruling the dead and living in complete darkness). In Ereshkigal's realm, the dead not only find rest, but many dark creatures do as well—such as demons.

---

22 Sirach. *The Alphabet of Ben Sira.* Valmadonna Trust Library, 1997. Part 78 mentions Lilith as Adam's first wife.

23 Frisvold, Nicholaj and Katy de Mattos. *The Canticles of Lilith.* Troy Books, 2022.

Lilith has been called a demon by some, connecting her to this chthonic realm. A specific type of demon from Mesopotamia are the *lilim*, or night spirits that feed on the life force of men in their sleep. Interestingly, in Ancient Greece, the term for a Witch was *strix*, which more specifically referred to a vampiric shapeshifting creature (usually taking the form of an owl) that screeched in the night and drank blood. Variations of this word can be found in Latin, such as *striga*, which roughly translates to "screecher." In modern Romanian, this same word means "barn owl." The word *strigoi*—referring to an undead, vampiric creature—stems from this root word as well. We even get the Italian word for Witch (*strega*) and sorcerer (*stregone*) from this same etymology relating to Lilithian mythos. Flight, albeit by astral means, has been associated with Witches for centuries. By some accounts, Lilith is considered to be the mother of Witch-blood, given her association with the current of darkness, isolated, wild places, and the reclamation of personal sovereignty.

China has a very long history of sorcerers and shamans who worked with a perfect balance of the elements, nature, and themselves. The common name for such practitioners was *wu;* they were capable of all sorts of skills such as divination, influencing the weather, healing, exorcising spirits from possessed people, and even masquerading as government officials.[24] In Japan, we see the concept of fox-employers, known as *kitsune-tsukai* or *kitsune-mochi*, depending on the region of Japan.[25] Their equivalent of the Witch mythos is more like shamanism, where practitioners commonly employed either foxes or snakes as familiars—the former being good, the latter being evil. Fox-employers were said to have a variety of powers, like shapeshifting and possessing people. In the Joseon dynasty of Korea, the art of magic was strictly monitored

24 Dashú, Max. "Wu: Ancient Female Shamans of Ancient China." Suppressed Histories, 2011, www.suppressedhistories.net/articles2/WuFSAC.pdf.

25 The Mythcrafts Team. "The Fox as Familiar: Japanese Witchcraft." Myth Crafts, 9 Aug. 2018, mythcrafts.com/2018/08/09/the-fox-as-familiar-japanese-witchcraft/.

by officials at court. In 1428, Crown Princess Hwi-bin Kim, consort of Munjong of Joseon, was deposed from her position and banished from court after it was discovered she'd casted love spells on her husband.[26]

Many traditional African religions—to this very day—place a heavy emphasis on developing change through rituals or magic; examples include the Yoruba and Igbo peoples of Nigeria. Famously, the ancient Egyptians had potent magic that has echoed for millennia, even influencing Western occultism as we know it. Isis, the great goddess of the pantheon, was said to have resurrected her husband, Osiris, after he was killed and dismembered by his brother, Set. The Caribbean, South and Central America have struggled to preserve indigenous practices, as many have not survived due to colonialism and the cultural erasure that resulted from it. Many newer religions have stemmed from syncretism—Santería in Cuba, Candomblé in Brazil, and Vodou in Haiti are all prime examples of established traditions that have set new roots.

Though this book is primarily written in the context of Witchcraft from Europe and New England, it is also beneficial to remember that many cultures around the world have their own systems for creating change through extraordinary means, even if they have another name or mythos behind it.

Our collective past as members of humanity provides lessons and inspiration for the present in which we live—and the future we create. If you feel the primal call of witchery, take action and dedicate yourself to this path. For those in covens and established traditions, initiation rituals are commonplace. If you do not have the privilege of being near one, a self-dedication is a great way to make this transition for yourself. The definition is in the name itself, as you are dedicating yourself to a path of transformation and power.

---

26 Wallace, Lorna. "10 Royals Who Dabbled in the Occult." *Listverse*, 17 Nov. 2022, listverse.com/2022/11/17/10-royals-who-dabbled-in-the-occult/.

A RITUAL OF SELF-DEDICATION

If you are hearing the call to the Old Craft, it is inevitable that you find yourself answering it. Below is a simple ritual of self-dedication to this path, way of life, and state of being. It's meant for outdoor use, but you may adapt it to an indoor setting. It will not require many tools at all—in fact, you're not likely to have many tools when you first begin practicing, as they are acquired over time (read more in Chapter Four, "Tools of the Trade").

Visit an isolated place out in nature during sunset. Any natural place will do so long as you are intuitively drawn to it. Be sure to identify a landmark near it, such as a tree or a specific stone. This is important not just for your safety, but because you may return to this place in the future to provide offerings and commune with the spirits that call the land home. Bring with you supplies to create a small bonfire, as well as a sterile medical lancet, a small shovel, some wine, and an offering. If you cannot consume alcohol, fruit juice or water will suffice. Be mindful of laws and regulations in your area about having bonfires in public, as you do not want to start a forest fire. The offering should be food—something sweet like baked goods or as simple as bread. Build your bonfire, then stand still with your eyes closed for the space of a few heartbeats. Take three deep breaths before opening your eyes. With feeling and dedication, say aloud:

> *Ancient spirits of all these lands, I ask for you to guide*
> *my hands. On this night and in this hour, I summon forth*
> *the most ancient of powers. I dedicate myself to the Craft*
> *of the Wise, aid me to ignite my inner flame and open*
> *my eyes! Ancient wise ones, by horn and by moon, I call*
> *you forth to commune and attune. Hail and welcome.*

Sit down before the bonfire, closing your eyes. Enter a meditative state. For those new to meditative practices, this can be done by simply closing your eyes. Take a few deep breaths. Clear your mind and let go of any feelings or thoughts that have nothing to do with this ritual. The Old Ones have their own ways of communicating with their Witches, and you will want to watch for one of their signs. You may have the ominous feeling that you are being watched by some unknown presence. You may also find yourself attracting the attention of some nearby wildlife who have taken a peculiar interest in your activities. Other unexplained natural phenomena may happen, and they may be so subtle that you don't realize what's happening in the moment, only for them to strike you as significant later. This is very normal.

Once you feel any of these sensations, ready your food and drink offering. Dig a small hole in the ground near the bonfire. Starting with the food, eat half of it and then recite:

This offering I share with you, Old Ones.
May I always be satisfied and abundant.

Put the other half before you and raise it up with reverence before putting it into the hole you dug. The significance of the hole is that it is an entryway into the world below and a way for your offerings to be accepted by that realm. Take the wine and sip half. Save the other half, raising the cup while saying:

This offering in which I partake, I also share with you,
Old Ones. May I always be satisfied and abundant.

Raise it with reverence like you did with the food, and then pour it into the hole you dug in the soil.

Lastly, take your sterile medical lancet and meditate on this very important act—by giving a few drops of your blood, you are giving of yourself to this path. This is for life; you cannot revoke it once it is complete. Prick your finger and squeeze enough blood out of it to smear onto the food you put into the earth. As your blood is smeared, say aloud:

> *By my blood, I dedicate myself to the Old Craft of the Wise. I open myself up to learning and growth, wisdom and understanding. I am led to the paths of pain and pleasure, creation and destruction, birth and death, betwixt and between, above and below. With my two hands, I shall reap both harmony and discord. With my eyes, I observe the natural world in its entirety. My inner fire is sparked; in my death, I find new life. I give thanks to you, Ancient Ones, for leading me to this very point in time and place. So mote it be.*

Put soil over the offerings you placed in the earth. Sit there at the bonfire, spending time out in nature. If you are indoors with a candle, your offerings can be buried after you spend time meditating on this journey you have just started. Feel and see yourself learning, growing, and changing. When you feel ready, end the ritual. If outdoors, put out the bonfire. If indoors, let the candle burn all the way down. When you go to sleep, be sure to make note of any dreams you have in relation to answering this primal call. This will be very telling.

Final Thoughts

Reading and researching are key to growth and development; experience is your best teacher. You may find that what you read in books is quite different than what you are perceiving when in an actual ritual setting. Take this mundane example: a new doctor in his residency spends many years in medical school and gets top grades, but during his first day on the job, he encounters a patient with an illness so rare that he's never heard of it. Thus, through this direct, firsthand experience, he is able to learn how to treat said patient for their ailment in the best way he can.

While it is a very good idea to learn about different cultures and their practices, it is *not* a good idea to cherry-pick. This is especially true when focusing on European magic. The Witchcraft we'll discuss in this book is European down to its core and should not necessarily cross over with anything else unless it suits your situation. For example, if you have personal, cultural ties to traditional Chinese shamanism and wish to incorporate it into your Craft *with* an appreciation and knowledge of its subject matter within the context of its tradition, feel free. If you are doing it because you think it's cool or just want to stand out, stop it. Doing so is highly disrespectful to that tradition, and if you have absolutely no idea what a particular practice means to someone else or their system, you should not be practicing it.

The same goes for closed traditions, that is, any tradition or system into which you have to be born or initiated in order to fully learn and master its mythos and practices. Several traditions of Witchcraft are only accessible to outsiders by initiation, and despite what most of the modern Witchcraft movement will tell you, these systems do have rules and methods, as well as reasons why they exist; one reason specifically is to provide a sense of structure for future generations of practitioners. That's why it's called a *system*. There should come a point in your relationship with the Craft where you find home in one path in all of its beauty—it being all you need. I implore you to pursue that.

CHAPTER THREE

THE ART OF MAGIC

As previously mentioned, magic has been practiced across the globe for millennia. Simply defined, magic is the art of manipulating energy in order to create change. In Witchcraft, magic is often done via spells and rituals; while they are two different means of raising energy, sometimes they go hand in hand. A *spell*, defined literally, is a means of enacting the effects of magic through the spoken word. Nowadays, this includes most kinds of magical workings, though charms or incantations help bind a spell by bringing intention into action. A *ritual* is a formalized process, often dictated by religious or spiritual practices, in which ceremonies are carried out according to a prescribed order. Examples of rituals that everyone can relate to include weddings, baptisms, graduations, and funerals. In the Old Craft, sometimes a spell is a part of a larger ritual. That being said, rituals should contain components or parts that have deep significance—otherwise, the operation is moot. In many traditions of the Craft, rituals are kept secret and sacred amongst the initiated members of their ranks.

Magic is an art that exists outside the boundaries of time and space; if anything, it is a way to manipulate the flow and fabric of time. When in a circle of art (read more on this in Chapter Five, "The Circle of Art and Sacred Spaces") or any liminal space, working a spell, raising power, and making your desires come true is much like taking the fabric of time and reweaving it to your design. A circle of art is a space between spaces where time is limitless, a meeting place between the realms of spirit and form to produce results—those results are that of your magic.

Contrary to what the media may show, magic is not an instantaneous art. Yes, sometimes spells can work sooner rather than later, but it is not like in *Harry Potter* where a wave of a wand and a flash of light creates an effect. Magic can take any amount of time to manifest in the physical world, and several factors influence this. One, your *proficiency*: are you a seasoned practitioner, having done enough spellwork to know what to expect and how to raise energy properly? If so, your success rate will likely be higher. If you are brand new to the practice and have only read one book, experience will be your best teacher—don't give up if your first spell or ritual doesn't work how you expected it to. If it eases any worries, please know that even experienced practitioners make mistakes and sometimes have spells not work in their favor. In the end, we are only human and bound to make errors.

The second factor is *attachment to the outcome*: are you overly worried about whether a spell is even going to manifest, let alone how you want it to? If so, you may not be successful. In doing magic and practicing the Old Craft as a whole, you are not only pouring your own energy into your workings, but any spirits present to aid you also lend theirs. If you keep worrying about the outcome, you're not only questioning your confidence and ability to perform magic, but you are also questioning the spirits you work with. How would you feel if you were being questioned and not trusted to do what you were asked to do, even though you're working very hard to make it happen? Pretty bad, I'm sure. All in all, trust your spirits and trust the process. Once it has been performed, let it manifest and forget about it. Reality will catch up in the way you have woven it.

The third thing to mention as a factor is your *choice of materials*—this may sound trivial given that material things are just objects, but as you will read later in Chapter Four, "Tools of the Trade," your tools and materials all have an innate spirit to them that you can interact with in order to manifest your magic. Choosing materials like herbs, for example, can affect your work greatly. If you are trying to gather herbs to create a candle dressing for a healing spell, choosing baneful herbs is the last thing you want to think about. Granted, most plant species on Earth have some medicinal properties no matter how poisonous they are, but in a spell where the idea is to create healing and restoration for someone sick or injured, using a baneful herb will literally kill that process. Another crucial thing to note is that, sometimes, you will come across a working that uses minimal tools or implements. In fact, I have done many simplistic spells and rituals without the need for tools such as my dagger. This is normal, but it is not an excuse to never use tools, as they can provide the powers of their own virtues to any work that you do. Thus, it is important to keep them on hand and cherish them. Choose your materials wisely, even if that means doing research on what you plan to use.

THE PYRAMID

A vital concept for any practitioner of magic to understand is the Witches' Pyramid, also known as the "Five Pillars of the Temple." This is a misnomer, as there are five points that make a pyramid—otherwise, it is merely a square. The Pyramid originates in Western occultism, particularly through the works of French occultist Éliphas Lévi.[27] Later, it became a part of the practices of the Hermetic Order of the Golden Dawn. Aleister Crowley, a famous figurehead from this order, later went on to influence early Wicca and even the earliest version of the Book of Shadows, given that he knew Gerald Gardner.[28]

---

27 Lévi, Éliphas, and Arthur Edward Waite, translator. *Transcendental Magic: Its Doctrine and Ritual.* Martino Fine Books, 2011.

28 Bogdan, Henrik. "The Influence of Aleister Crowley on Gerald Gardner and the Early Witchcraft Movement." Brill, 1 Jan. 2009.

This is why we find the Witches' Pyramid among Witchcraft circles today. It outlines five basic philosophies that lead to effective magical practice—*to know, to dare, to will,* to *keep silent,* and *to go.*[29]

1. **To know (Latin: *noscēre*)** instructs that you gain knowledge about what you are doing, why you're doing it, or how to go about doing it. Otherwise, how can you be successful? Knowledge is power, so let it be yours.

2. **To dare (Latin: *audēre*)** reminds us to be fearless in what we are doing and to not let doubts, misgivings, or a lack of confidence hold you back. Otherwise, how can you expect to be successful? Facing and overcoming one's fears is a major transformation for many Witches, offering an extremely liberating outcome. A foundation of knowledge is where a journey begins, not where it ends; ignorance fuels fear, so it is important to use the asset of knowledge to dispel our fears, anxieties, and doubts.

3. **To will (Latin: *velle*)** means to have the drive and conviction to do what you're planning. If you have no will to do something, or if you question your desires, how can you expect to be successful? Know what you desire and what your true intentions are before carrying anything out. When you do something, you put your all into it; no more, no less. To say you will *try* implies there is a possibility of failure. If you have the idea of failure in your mind, you will not be successful.

4. **Keeping silent (Latin: *tacēre*)** is probably the second-most important point on the Pyramid, as it entails keeping silent about your secrets and your magic. If you share knowledge too freely, you lose it; you may consciously remember how to do something, but if you tell someone how to do what you know how to do, it's bound to be

---

29 Chauran, Alexandra. "Understanding Elementals." *Llewellyn Worldwide,* 11 Nov. 2013, www.llewellyn.com/journal/article/2399.

lost in translation. Plus, there's a huge chance they won't understand something so archaic. So, keep your mouth shut; reveal nothing to people you don't trust. This also extends to the Internet and social media—there is a vast community, now, that loves to share photos of their workings and processes just for clout, validation, or to prove they can do something extraordinary. This is a terrible idea—if you share your work with others, even a photo on your social media, someone can use that against you or interfere with your work. In many traditions of the Old Craft, silence is sacred, as it preserves the sanctity of rituals and practices unique to said tradition. If the oath of silence taken at initiation is broken in any way, the consequences can be dire.

5. **To go (Latin: *ire*)** is the most important aspect of the Pyramid, represented by the top point. With everything else in perfect synergy and balance, you should be ready to go and do your magic. Put that will into action and send it out!

KARMIC RETURN AND BACKFIRING DEBUNKED

Karma is an idea from Eastern philosophies like Buddhism, but we also see more fundamental interpretations in Hinduism. Both interpretations are similar and relate to reincarnation. *Karma* is defined as the sum of all the things someone does in their current incarnation and any previous ones, which determines their fate in future incarnations. Karma, in a fundamental Buddhist definition, equates to "action." This does not constitute as *what goes around, comes around,* but rather, *what happens, happens.* The former of these is the result of Western culture twisting the meaning of something it doesn't collectively understand.

The Threefold Law, as seen in Wicca, is a perfect example of how karma's true meaning was distorted. It states that whatever you do comes back to you three times. However, it is an incredibly illogical and flawed way of thinking. First off, energy cannot multiply, disappear, or get destroyed; it simply changes form. In physics, this is called "the law of conservation of energy." The former piece of dogma also doesn't measure up to Newton's third law: "with every action, there is an equal and opposite reaction." That being said, if *you* are the reaction when someone severely wrongs you, does that make you deserve punishment—even if you are in the right? How will anything coming back three times help you? If you really think about it, you'll find that this concept is completely useless in the practice of Witchcraft.

Gerald Gardner, the founder of Wicca, created the Three-fold Law to make the predominantly Christian world calm down about magic. On this basis, Wicca is no different from most other religions, in that it has dogma for adherents to follow. Of course, many modern Wiccans that do not belong to an established tradition within the religion misconstrue this Threefold Law and take it to mean that they should only do *good* or *light* works. This is why you see many who are new think that there is one right way to do something, and because of their conditioning in their prior religion, they lean more toward the light aspects rather than the flipside of the coin. In actuality, limiting your learning and practice to just the light is anything but positive—light can blind, just as darkness can obscure the truth. Learning about both is key to achieving spiritual equilibrium.

This most certainly does not mean a Witch has free reign to do what they want; just because you *can* do something, it does not mean you *should*. For example, it can be agreed on by many that it is unacceptable, and even a bit ridiculous, to hex someone who squints at you. A Witch must know the consequences of their actions and be fully prepared to take on any responsibilities for what they do or send out. If you do something, something *will* happen, and whether or not it affects you will depend on your intentions. I get asked a lot whether spells backfire—those aspiring to cast a spell for the first time are often afraid of just that. In my own experience, the phenomenon of backfiring happens not because of the spell itself, but because of external factors that are either beyond your control or went unconsidered.

The latter of these is important to note because you may have a seemingly perfect spell in its planning and execution, only for a surprise to come out of the woodwork as your results begin to manifest. You may experience anything in this case, depending on what you did, from an unpleasant loss to an enlightening epiphany. The key to dealing with backlash from a working is to separate yourself from the outcome, including the process itself. A tried-and-true way to do this is to emotionally cut yourself off from the outcome, knowing full well that what you sent out will manifest in its own time. If personal cost is in the equation, you have the understanding and wisdom to realize that some risk may be required for your desire to come true. In my experience, this risk can manifest as a loss of something in your life. As the universe balances itself out, something you love may be offered up as a metaphorical sacrifice. And perhaps that sacrifice was *meant* to happen, because you put in the energy for something to happen—nature is just taking what's hers.

Many modern Witches have colloquially viewed their own powers as karma itself or believed themselves able to control such a force through spells. However, this perspective is flawed, and one reason why power trips and delusions start. In certain situations, you may view your magic as karma, but that does not make you above the natural laws of the universe. You are not God; you are an *extension* of divinity living in a human body, given the obligation of discerning when to use the power given to you and whether it is needed at all. Everything has personal cost, whether we want it to happen or not, because in the end, the natural order must restore itself.

Intention, Action, and Direction

A very common notion in the modern Witchcraft community is that intention is everything. Some practitioners may find this to be true, but based on my experiences, I do not. Magic is so much more than intention; it is also action and direction. Yes, intention is important, but it is nothing without being backed by action and driven forward in a specific direction. Think of this in the following order:

- **Intention** is the initial thought or idea that leads you to doing magic in the first place. It is clear and thought-out, used to select implements and plan your ritual or spell.
- **Action** comes next; this is where you put intention into action by channeling it into your working. Action is also literal here; anything involving physical movements, spoken word, dances, drumming, and so on are all considered action.
- **Direction** is last. This is when the raised power is directed at the objective so it can manifest within the realms. Then reality catches up, and your spell has come true.

Intention is not everything—take a few mundane examples. You may *intend* to go to the salon for a new cut-and-color, but are you actually going to *go?* If not, nothing has happened. The intention of going to the salon is just in your mind and represents nothing more; there is nothing to show for this intention because your hair is still a bit too long and that same color. This principle can be applied to spellwork and rituals.

Helpful Magical Techniques

Affirmations are written or spoken statements intended to bring a desired change into one's life. While an affirmation can be made for any purpose, they are always structured with positive, can-do language. This means words like *no* or *can't* are not included in their creation. This is because you are commanding your will into life, bringing it into manifestation. Think back to the Pyramid—to *try* implies the possibility of failure, and if failure is in your mind, your desire will not come to fruition.

It is the same idea with using *no* in an affirmative sentence. Using the word *no* or any of its forms (such as *don't, can't,* or *won't*) also has the opposite effect, as magic tends to take the path of least resistance; meaning, it can attract exactly what you are trying to repel or get rid of. When commanding your will, you must do it with full intention and full awareness of your desire in its purest form. Use your voice as the ultimate tool of reaching into the other worlds; when speaking your spells, chants, or incantations, speak with conviction and power. Speak your will into existence with every syllable, vowel, and inflection. Remember, *you* are the one in control of most things happening within your space. Finding your voice is one of the key things to do when first starting out. It may take time, but when you have the sense and confidence to speak with clarity and power, the rest will follow.

Being able to focus on a spell or ritual is vital. You must work your magic in an environment where you can focus fully on the task at hand—try to avoid distractions like the TV or your phone. When working a spell, it is like your sense of time completely stops; this is especially true if you are working in a circle or other liminal space. Even without one, though, it is important to stay focused. Focus goes hand in hand with visualization, for if you can clearly imagine the spellwork coming to life in your mind while working, it's a sign that some successful magic is going to be produced. There are many techniques to improve visualization; I find that, being a visual person myself, I can picture details quite well. For those keen on learning by reading or listening, this technique may take some time to fully master. The following technique combines most of the above skills important for working magic.

Find a simple object—perhaps an apple or an orange—and place it in front of you on a table. Something simple works best when attempting this exercise for the first time. Clear your mind and relax in any way that works for you—take a hot bubble bath, do breathwork, light some appealing incense. Close your eyes and take a few deep breaths before concentrating on the details of the object. Take in its scent, texture, color, and any unique markings on its surface. You can even take it in your hand to feel it briefly. Try to commit as many details as possible to memory before setting the object back down and closing your eyes.

Now, try to call forth an image of the object in your mind's eye, recalling as much detail as you possibly can. Hold this image for about thirty seconds. When ready, release the image and open your eyes, looking down at the object. Is it exactly as you imagined it to be? Don't be discouraged if you get it a little wrong, even the first time—it takes practice to attune your mind's eye to your surroundings. You may want to continue practicing but with even more detailed objects, or you could go bigger with places or people. In magic, you will often work towards targets that require visualization skills, so it's a very important skill to have—even in the development of certain psychic abilities, which will be covered in a future chapter.

SYMPATHETIC MAGIC

A traditional way to work magic on a target is by means of sympathetic magic. This time-honored magical technique utilizes what are known as taglocks. These are items that serve as a direct link to the person a spell is meant to affect. Common taglocks include hair, skin parings, nail clippings, blood, clothing, photographs, and even handwriting. Sympathetic magic, which uses a *like affects like* philosophy, may also consist of obtaining a personal belonging of theirs to use in workings. This also could be an item with special meaning to not only the person, but the result of the spell. Sympathetic magic is an ancient form of working magic that still is extremely effective today.

I must warn you: *do not* handle foreign bodily fluids without protective gear such as gloves. Also, bear in mind that magic performed with body fluids such as blood can be permanent. This is because blood is our very essence at its core, symbolic of the red thread that connects us all to our collective ancestry. Urine is another bodily fluid that has been used over time, as it has cleansing properties and is sterile. People used to do laundry and brighten their clothes with old urine, which turned into ammonia; this chemical is still used for modern-day cleaning. There is historical evidence that one implement in crafting a Witch bottle—especially the Bellarmine, a variety of jar from seventeenth century England—was urine. Hair was also used in these bottles, as it was a form of sympathetic magic on the self. When these bottles were completed, they were buried under the thresholds of one's home for protection. Another example is the hanging of poppets inside a chimney to represent all the members of a family. The chimney—as well as windows and doors—was seen as a means for Witches to come into a house using their spirit form. These poppet decoys were crafted to absorb any malefic forces directed at any one member of the family.

Sympathetic magic has many versatile uses, whether for healing or destruction. The key is to not only have some kind of a link to your target, but to *feel* and *see* it happening in real time. If you are trying to rid someone's body of disease, *see* and *feel* the person in perfect, radiant health, running around and skipping in the sunshine. If you are trying to cause harm, *see* and *feel* the target withering away like a decaying flower. Visualization is a great tool to use in any working, and sympathetic magic is no exception.

OTHER TIPS FOR WORKING

If candles are to be used for a working, let them always be virgin. By this, I mean unused or purified. Purifying a candle is as simple as running it under water or fumigating it with a purifying incense such as frankincense, sandalwood, or myrrh. Church incense is also a great choice. It is a bad idea to reuse candles from previous workings for several reasons. One is quite obvious, as when you reuse a candle imbued with virtues and power meant for a different kind of spell, it can greatly interfere with your working's result. Second, it is a great idea to let candles completely burn down even after a ritual is closed; it is a sign of completion.

Collecting crystals and gemstones makes for a nice hobby, and most modern practitioners have gotten work done with them, yet they are not always a necessity. They are especially useful on things you can wear, such as jewelry, charged for any purpose. It is no secret that certain gems can draw properties to the wearer: examples being carnelian for good health, amethyst for sobriety, or jasper for protection. However, you do not need crystals or gems for every single working.

Chapter Four

Tools of the Trade

Mechanics, plumbers, and surgeons all have one thing in common—they have tools of the trade that help get the job done. Witches are no different. We use tools that serve us in manifesting our will into reality. In the end, it is up to you what tools you feel drawn to use in your practice. Some spells call for barely any tools at all. There are many possibilities for what tools can be made of, and how they ultimately affect magical workings. It is not uncommon for traditional practitioners to have multiples of a certain tool for different purposes. A good example is if you keep two wands of different woods: one of peach-wood for acts of blessing, and one of yew to connect with the dead. An example from my own practice is keeping two separate mortar and pestles—one for work with ingestible herbs and the other for poisonous ones—to prevent cross-contamination. When you begin to cast spells, keep in mind that the materials you gather depend on the type of spell you are doing as well as the intent. These are called *correspondences,* which we will get to later in this book. Here are some of the most common ritual tools used in magic:

- **Dagger:** Many modern-day practitioners call this an *athame.* The dagger serves to conduct and send out energy. It is a common misconception that the dagger is not used to cut anything physical. Daggers were created for that very purpose, be it cutting cords or carving symbols into candles because at the end of the day, that is what they are—knives. However, in many traditions, it is understood that the dagger is not to be used in that way. You can use it to cast a circle, as it *carves out* the air in which the circle sits, as well as to ward off harmful, unwanted influences, spirits, and interference as a magical weapon of sorts. It can be argued that a magical tool gains more power the more it is used, even if it is a ritual knife used for cutting things or defending your work. The white-handled knife, called the *boline,* is reserved for the harvesting of herbs or cutting of cords. In symbolic sexual union, the dagger represents the masculine aspect, as it is inserted into the chalice, another ritual tool. The dagger corresponds to the Fire or Air elements. Heat forges a blade, and when used as a spiritual weapon or to conduct energy, it is often held in the air.

- **Cauldron:** One of the Witch's more well-known tools, the cauldron serves a variety of purposes in Witchcraft. It is usually made of cast-iron, but you can also find them made from other materials such as copper or brass. As a vessel, the cauldron can be used to hold charcoal over which to burn incense. It can also hold water, fire, a candle, or serve as a safe container for burning objects. The cauldron is a symbol of transformation and rebirth, and is a feminine object, representing the womb in several pre-Christian cultures, particularly that of the Ancient Celts.[30] Whatever goes into the cauldron never comes out the same way, as it is a tool used to birth your work into physical existence. It represents the element Water.

- **Chalice:** Also known as "the cup," the chalice is another magical tool associated with femininity. This tool is traditionally made of metals

---

30 Cartwright, Mark. "Gundestrup Cauldron." *World History Encyclopedia*, 15 Feb. 2021, www.worldhistory.org/Gundestrup_Cauldron/.

like silver or an organic substance like horn,[31] but it is not uncommon to see ones made of bone, ceramic, or glass. It holds libations to be consumed and offered to any spirits present in a ritual, commonly wine. Sometimes a chalice contains consecrated water to purify spaces and objects. The chalice is a symbol in religions such as Christianity, where it is known as the Holy Grail, the very cup used by Joseph to collect Christ's blood as he was crucified. The chalice also represents the female in symbolic sexual union, receiving the dagger. Like the cauldron, the chalice represents the element Water.

- **Wand:** The wand is another well-known tool, and it is described as the extension of one's arm. Wands are used for directing and channeling energy outward into the ether. They have long been used in ceremonial magic in addition to the staff, which serves a similar purpose with the only difference being its size. Wands or staves can be made of a variety of woods depending on the intention. Ash is the most traditional for wands. The wand is a masculine tool and corresponds with the Air element. That said, in tarot, it is often depicted representing the Fire element.

- **Stang:** The stang is a double-pronged staff used by some traditions of the Old Craft to serve as a focal point for rituals—and even as a mobile altar—especially those involving the Horned One. It can also represent the World Tree, a conduit between the world below and the sky above to aid in sending your power in these directions if need be. The bottom of a stang is usually shod with an iron nail to help concentrate and fix the power raised to the area in which you or your group are working. Depending on the time of year, a stang can be decorated, but one common feature with all stangs is the place between the prongs

---

31 Huson, Paul. *Mastering Witchcraft.* G.P. Putnams, 1970.

where a candle can sit, emblematic of the flame of enlightenment that sits between the Horned God's tines. Lastly, the stang can assist with spirit journeying. The stang does not actually have a formal elemental designation, but since it is an intermediary between worlds, Spirit seems appropriate here.

- **Broom:** Also known as a *besom*, the broom is one of the first things people think about when they hear the word *Witch*. Brooms can be used in the original, practical sense, like for brushing away debris from the floor. However, they can also be used to purify an area of unwanted energies and influences. Brooms are heavily associated with spirit flight. In short, spirit flight is the journey made out-of-body (in spirit form), either with the help of psychoactive substances (such as a flying ointment), meditation, or deep dream states. In a traditional circle, the broom goes in the northeast, serving as an entryway for anyone set to be present in a working. The broom corresponds to Air and Earth, with a bi-gender association: the handle being masculine and the bristles being feminine.

- **Paten:** The paten is a tile upon which to charge objects used for magic. There are many symbols you can have as your paten, such as the pentacle—or you can have a plain ceramic dish. Aside from being a tile on which to charge items, it can be used to present offerings to spirits you work with. This tool corresponds to the Earth element.

- **Jewelry:** Jewelry is a prime example of personal adornment for many people. For a Witch, however, wearing jewelry serves a much deeper purpose than just looking good. In fact, it doesn't have to be shown off at all. A Witch's jewelry items are vessels of power that, if charged, draw a variety of influences to the wearer. The most common type of jewelry is that worn for protection or luck—qualities sought out by practitioners and non-practitioners alike. Jewelry can include various gemstones that are meaningful to the wearer. Witches often wear pieces like rings, bracelets, earrings, and pendants.

OTHER SUPPLIES

Indispensable sundries for the magic practitioner include candles, incense, herbs, stones, and divination tools. It is a very good idea to have different kinds of candles on hand. Keep in mind the size of your candles so that they last for as long as you are doing a working, especially if it is one you are performing over the course of a few days to a week. Incenses come in stick and cone varieties, but it's best to create your own blends from herbs and oils to add potency to your workings—dealing with the virtues of different plants. Loose or resin-based incense needs to be burned over charcoal. For most charcoal disks, you will need sand underneath the disks in a firesafe bowl, and you have to light it and wait until it becomes white; this means it is hot enough to burn the blend effectively.

Another important thing to have is a way to purify yourself, your tools, or your working space. In most cases, having consecrated salt and water works well. Salt is a natural preservative, but also a repellant. It can be utilized to purify objects and places. When purifying a place with salt, sprinkle it about and let it sit for a few minutes before sweeping it up. With it, sweep away all of the unwanted or negative energies, and then throw it in the trash. One of my favorite ways to purify objects—especially for ritual use—is by having a bowl of salt and putting the object in it for a few days so that the salt absorbs any impurities it may hold. When it comes to herbs, buying them dried in starter packs is a good start, but eventually you may want to forage your own, learning about your local flora and actively working with it. In fact, the latter is something I highly encourage because there is no better teacher than experience, especially with the spirits of the plants you work with. It goes without saying that as you progress, you will find yourself becoming more creative with what you use in magic, especially if doing something in a pinch.

Below is a simple consecration procedure for purposing your magical tools for your practice. You can use it to empower your dagger, besom, cauldron, cup, or any other ritual tool that can aid your magic. The elemental associations of the directions used are heavily inspired by the English method of the Circle of Art, which greatly differs from the classical Western associations where east is Air, south is Fire, west is Water and north is Earth. I provide more of an explanation on why this is in Chapter Five, "The Circle of Art and Sacred Spaces."

MATERIALS

- A small container of spring water
- A small container of salt
- A white candle
- Sandalwood incense
- The tool you wish to consecrate
- Three drops of blood (a sterile diabetic lancet is recommended for this; be sure to properly dispose of it when finished)

INSTRUCTIONS

This procedure is best performed when the moon is full or new. Set aside a time where you can sit in peace and quiet. Choose a location where you will not be disturbed. Take three full deep breaths, getting yourself into a relaxed state of mind.

With all of this out in front of you, take the tool in both of your hands and look at it. Recite the following:

> *I summon all of the powers within and without,*
> *Above and below, before and behind me,*
> *To aid me in consecrating this tool for use in my Craft.*

May this (name of tool here) *serve
me well in all endeavors.*

Hold the tool over the incense. Watch as the smoke rises up to meet the tool and imagine it purifying the object of any energies that were there before. As you visualize this, recite:

*In the name of the northern guardians,
Domain of the dark winds of spirit,
I consecrate, bless, and empower this* (tool).

Next, hold the tool over the flame of the candle. Be careful if the tool happens to be metal, like a piece of jewelry or your dagger—you do not want it to melt. Hold it just above the flame at a distance where it can be warmed rather than overheat. As you imagine the heat purifying the object of any prior energies, recite:

*In the name of the eastern guardians,
Domain of the fiery serpent,
I consecrate, bless, and empower this* (tool).

Now, take the tool to the salt and sprinkle a few pinches over it, imagining the solidity of the salt cleansing and stabilizing the process. As you do, recite:

*In the name of the southern guardians,
Domain of ancient stone,
I consecrate, bless, and empower this* (tool).

At this stage, the water should be in a designated container. Natural materials, such as shell or bone, are best. However, anything will work in a pinch. If the tool is metal, you do not want for it to rust, and you'll likewise need to be careful if the object you are consecrating is wooden, like a wand. In these cases, sprinkle water over the surface of the item. Otherwise, simply dip the object into the container, and imagine the cleansing properties of the water removing any energy that was there before. Recite:

In the name of the western guardians,
Domain of the deepest seas,
I consecrate, bless, and empower this (tool).

For the last step, bring the tool closer to you and take three deep breaths, exhaling onto the object. By doing this, you are breathing life into the object you are consecrating. With each exhale, feel that the tool is becoming imbued with life, the spirit within the object awakening. Then, set it down on your workspace and procure three drops of blood from your right index finger with the lancet. Be mindful of your health and safety—always use *sterile* equipment if you need to draw blood. The last thing you need is an infection or injury resulting from carelessness. Let a few drops of blood make contact with the tool, reciting three times in succession:

By my breath and blood, you are sanctified.
(Tool), *you are mine. Serve me well.*
So it is done.

Keep your tools in a safe place, ideally away from prying eyes. Sheath any blades you may use in your spellwork.

An important thing to remember is that tools gain strength and power over time, the more you use them. Thus, I encourage you to start using them as soon as possible once they are dedicated for use. With regards to the consecration procedure above, repeat it as often as you feel you need to in order to keep your tools—and the spirits that vibrate within them—happy and fulfilled. By doing this, you are also reminding your tools of their use and service to you as the practitioner.

As a final note, it is important to remember that each and every one of your tools has an essence to it. They are not just objects or tools—they are extensions of *you*, and with every use, they will only become more potent. Each tool has an innate spirit; may they serve you well.

Keeping a Record

Historically speaking, most practitioners passed down their magical knowledge and wisdom by word of mouth. It was unlikely that the common person even had the educational training to read, let alone keep detailed journals of magical lore. If there was anyone who could read and write proficiently, it would have been the clergy, who kept records of sacred texts and any ceremonies they performed. Even before the establishment of the Catholic Church, this was the case. In Old Norse society, only the völvur and goði knew how to interpret the Futhark; the masses could not.[32] It is because of this restrictive form of education—and the establishment of churches—that we have lost a lot of information to history.

Despite the regulations the Catholic Church put on people's behavior, this did not stop ceremonial magic (mostly influenced from practices brought from the Middle East) from being performed and recorded in what are known as *grimoires:* books that contain magical procedures. The more famous grimoires which are still renowned to this day include *Clavicula Salomonis* (*The Key of Solomon the King*), *The Lemegeton*, the *Sixth and Seventh Books of Moses*, *Black Pullet*, *Grimorium Verum*, the *Grimoire of Armadel*, and *The Red Dragon*. The idea of the grimoire has been taken into the modern era. For instance, in the 1950s, Wicca became legalized and therefore more public, and the

---

32 McKay, Andrew. "Viking Runes: The Historic Writing Systems of Northern Europe." Life in Norway, 21 Aug. 2020, www.lifeinnorway.net/viking-runes/.

term *Book of Shadows* was invented by Gerald Gardner, as he needed a name for the religious texts of Wicca. This is, in a way, a grimoire because it contains instructions for the rituals of the Wiccan religion in addition to its liturgy.

For an individual practitioner, it is a very good idea to keep a record of your magic and your path. This record can be called a *Book of Shadows*, as mentioned above, but other terms include *spellbook*, *liber umbrārum et lux* (Latin for "book of shadows and light"), or simply *journal* or *book*. You can also use the term *grimoire*; even though this word once referred to an instruction manual of magical procedures, it has been redefined as any magical book including one that a Witch keeps as a personal record. In the same vein of Witchcraft-related folklore from Europe, you can even call it a *black book*. It depends on your tradition or personal preference. For practicality's sake, it may be convenient for you to begin with a simple notebook or composition book to document anything you find important, as well as any magic you do and the results. In the beginning, you won't really know how to write your own spells, so you're likely to get them from books or online. Keep a collection of these to get a feel for how spells are written and laid out; they will be handy later.

Here is a brief list of things you could include in your personal grimoire:

- **Spells** (and their outcomes)
- **Rituals** (and any results that come during or after the fact)
- **Correspondences:** Lists of the different properties and virtues of things like plants, stones, metals, woods, times of day, seasons, moon phases, and so on.
- **Recipes:** Anything from your own healing tincture to that special soup you make when a family member is ill so that they recover more quickly.
- **Astrology:** Witches have always had an uncanny connection to the stars and cosmic bodies; why not include information about it in your personal grimoire?

- **Divination:** Any methods you use, your findings, and their results.
- **Artwork:** Such as decorations, fancy fonts, or pictures inspired by visions and astral journeys.
- **Relevant lore:** Any interesting local lore in your area that you want to acknowledge as part of your Craft; incorporating all things local to you is essential.
- **Familiar spirits:** This is covered later in the book in the chapter *Familiar Spirits*, but Witches tend to have spirit helpers; include yours in the grimoire's pages.
- **Cleansing and exorcism procedures:** Two of the most important arts you will learn on this path, spiritual hygiene and ridding places, objects, and even people of unwanted residuals.
- **Tenets and philosophies:** These can be individual, part of your tradition, or both! Don't be afraid to evolve over time, though, and look back on what you thought a few years ago. This is how we grow as practitioners and people.

As time passes, you may want to keep separate journals for different topics. You may have your primary book, but have another form of documentation for dreams, astral journeys, recipes, correspondences, and other things just to keep organized. You may elect to keep a binder with tabbed divider and sheet protectors with a section for each topic and have that serve as your primary book. Of course, if you find yourself a mentor or get initiated into a tradition, you will need to conform to their guidelines and rules—limiting as they may be. When it is just you, however, it's okay to take as many liberties as you want. Be creative! I have had pages of my personal workings decorated in drawings, calligraphy, and other such adornments that really made the book my own. It is always nice and empowering to look and see a bit of *you* on the same page where you wrote a spell's procedure and outcome. Use discretion in who you share your book with. In some cases, especially if you are part of a tradition or stream of practice, sharing your book's contents is taboo.

Writing your own spells is a very powerful thing you can do as a Witch because it affords you the opportunity to personalize your magic. It takes a lot of thought and knowledge about magic, correspondences, and controlling the powers within and without to make it happen, but it is worth it in the end to have something you can call your own versus a spell you found online. When crafting your own spells (directions for which can be found in Chapter Eleven, "Practical Spellcraft") you may find it convenient to keep a separate notebook to draft them out, and then copy them into your book when you are certain they've manifested. When writing your own spells, it is okay if it's nothing but chicken scratch—don't be afraid to have multiple drafts of a spell.

FINAL THOUGHTS

Don't stress if you do not have many tools or have trouble finding the perfect tools. Tools will always make their way to the person they are destined for. If you feel drawn to (and have the skill to) do so, you can even craft your own tools. Many occult suppliers carry a wide array of magical tools to use in their Craft. The important thing is to select tools you are drawn to. I recommend physically going to a shop, and if you are able, feeling the tool in your hand. Get a sense of how it may serve you. Take a few moments with it. You may feel an intuitive pull, or you may not. Only you can tell if a tool is meant for you.

Many people like to visit antique shops or consignment stores for tools, which is a fine idea except for the fact that many of the items offered in these shops have a history. Use caution when getting anything from an antique or consignment shop— and trust your gut. If it feels like something may be attached to the tool you've put your hand on, do not bring it home. This is especially true for mirrors, which are said to be portals. If you manage to get something from an antique or consignment shop to use as a magical tool, make sure you cleanse it a little extra before you dedicate it for use. You can do this by leaving it out in the moonlight, leaving it in a bowl of salt for up to three days at a time, or fumigating it with the smoke of such botanicals as angelica.

CHAPTER FIVE

THE CIRCLE OF ART AND SACRED SPACES

C ircles have been an integral part of magic for centuries; even older are sacred spaces. Around the world, many ancient ruins of temples and groves are evidence of humanity holding not just spiritual practices sacred, but the places in which they were held. The general purpose that circles and sacred spaces have in common is that they lie *in between worlds*. It's a space where the seen and unseen unite to help you alter the course from the very point in time from which you work. Time also passes differently in these spaces, as they integrate all three aspects of time—past, present, and future—simultaneously. The formal term for *a space between spaces* is "liminal space." Therefore, when you prepare an area for a magical working or ritual, you are dedicating it as a place in between the realms of spirit and form, so that they unite in perfect synergy and harmony for the work to take place.

The most prominent historical examples of circles are those seen in ceremonial magic, particularly *Clavicula Salomonis* and *Grimorium Verum*, but they also have made their way into the mainstream with Thelema, Wicca, and other spiritual paths. To the practitioners of old, nature was sacred but also feared and respected; in the same place you foraged for nuts or berries, a bear could maul you. When working with spiritual entities, it has been argued that it is antithetical to use a circle for protection when you are delving into gray territory to begin with. This argument adds that when working with spirits, a circle of protection can actually keep out those with whom you're trying to work with. However, there is an exception. It's a famous magic circle used in the evocation of angelic or demonic entities, which includes a triangle of containment as seen in Solomonic grimoires and Kabbalistic practices.

Magic circles are a good thing to know about in the event that you need to use one, but it is important to be mindful that they are not required for *all* the magic you work and send out. For the most part, purifying your workspace and dedicating it is enough to sanctify it, especially if the work is being done in your home. Regular upkeep of your sacred space, such as physical cleaning, cleansing, and purifying are all devotional acts in themselves. More involved or lengthy workings or rituals should be performed with a circle cast. These include but are not limited to spirit work, Sabbats, rites of communion with ancestors or the Old Ones, group workings, and initiations or self-dedications. This is because a circle is a space between spaces, a world between worlds, meant to contain all of the energies raised within, as well as keep out any unwanted or harmful interference, spirits, or energy. For instance, if you have more than one participant in your ritual, you'll want to not only protect them from outside forces but contain everything you are working for them. How you cast your Circle of Art also depends on the work you're doing. If it is constructive, tread clockwise starting in the north and moving west. If it is destructive, tread counterclockwise starting north and ending in the east.

You may find that this book's method for casting a circle differs from the mainstream way of doing so, as it is heavily inspired by English traditional magic. We'll harness the four classical elements—aspects of the natural world—for our magic and rituals. They consist of Earth, Air, Fire, and Water, all possessing their own virtues. In magic, elemental correspondences are tied to many things such as zodiac signs, herbs, gems, and much more. Instead of the Air element corresponding to the east, it is situated in the north. On a compass, north points to a place where the wind blows cold; the closer to the North Pole you are, the less likely it is to find any sort of life for miles. The Fire element has its home in the east instead of the south due to the rising sun, a ball of plasma in space that provides Earth with warmth and light. Earth—rather than being in the north— is in the south because she (Earth) is below our feet. In this version of a circle casting, your back is facing the south, which is opposite to the north. Yet, one thing remains the same—water stays in the west, the direction of sunset. This is a much more literal way of associating the elements with cardinal directions.

Each element has a magical property attached to it, which can enhance your magical workings and their outcomes. In the north, you can find help with spirit work, divination, destruction, and binding. Let the bright fires of the east lend their power to workings of enlightenment, strength, protection, and sexuality. Turn behind you to the south to find assistance with workings of wealth, abundance, physical healing, fertility, the virtues of plants, and your ancestors. Where the moon controls the waters of the west, face it to receive added potency in sea magic, dreams, emotional or mental healing, and cleansing. This is by no means a complete list—let the circle and its virtues teach you!

Personal Preparation

Preparation is key to working any spell or ritual—bathe before-hand, meditate to get your mind in a clear state, and listen to some music that motivates you. Right before casting your Circle of Art, you may even anoint your brow, palms, throat, heart area, lower abdomen, knees, and feet as a means of preparation. If you're working with a group, this can be done to open up the energy centers within the body so that you can begin as an active participant. Aside from literal meditation, activities that evoke a meditative state like knitting or embroidery also help prepare your mind for what is to come.

In many occult texts with complex procedures, such as *The Book of the Sacred Magic of Abramelin the Mage*, there is mention of deprivation to prepare oneself for a spiritual undertaking. This is symbolic of self-sacrifice in order to gain spiritual attunement; fasting and abstinence have been used to do so for centuries. In the example text mentioned, there are many extreme measures of deprivation and restrictions that are said to help the practitioner get the most out of the workings within. However, times have changed, and we have a better understanding of health.

I do *not* recommend fasting if you have a history of an eating disorder. As for having sacramental drink, I am all for replacing wine with juice or another beverage if you have a history of substance abuse and wish to maintain your sobriety. Maybe you just don't like alcohol—that's fine too. Do not compromise your health or well-being with such things; your recovery is much more important. I do not feel it is mandatory for every single working to have some sort of deprivation accompanying it, but if you feel the need to do so, choose something that will not affect your health. Some ideas in the modern world include not watching TV for a day, not eating ice cream up to four hours before your working is set to begin, or not spending money for an entire day. Be creative, especially if this is something you wish to incorporate in your practice as a means of self-preparation.

CREATING A CIRCLE OF ART

Find a place where you won't be disturbed, either out in nature or in your own home. Start by physically clearing the space of anything that should not be there or that has nothing to do with your ritual. Take your besom and ritually sweep the space, starting in the north and making your way clockwise. Physically cleaning your room beforehand is a bonus. When this is done, lay your besom diagonally in the northeast of the circle, the traditional entryway of the Circle of Art. This is especially important if your ritual has multiple participants, as they'll need some way to get into the space.

Place your tools in their associated cardinal direction. The dagger, for example, goes in the east. A bell and incense would go in the north. Blessed water goes in the west along with sacramental drink in the chalice and your cauldron, kept empty to contain potential ingredients for the task at hand. You could even use the cauldron as a vessel to contain blessed water. Stones, the paten, and sacramental food go in the south. Going back to blessed water, it can be made simply by combining water with a pinch of salt, stirring it with the blade of your dagger, and creating the sign of the cross over it, saying aloud:

> *I consecrate and bless this water in the Old Ones' name,*
> *so that this place be cleansed and blessed by them.*

Sprinkle this as you tread three times around the circle; the solution you created represents both Water and Earth (salt). Then, take the candle from the east as you tread three more times around. Lastly, take the incense around the circle in the same fashion, treading three times before putting it back in the north of the circle. Once finished, recite the following:

> *By Earth, Air, Fire and Water, this*
> *circle is purified and blessed.*

Now, it is time to call each elemental domain to lend their power to your ritual. Begin in the north, facing it with your right arm raised, palm up. Recite:

> *I summon and call upon the black spirits of*
> *the north, powers of wind and air.*
> *Hear my call—and be here with me!*

Call the east in the same fashion; facing that direction with your arm raised, recite:

> *I summon and call upon the red spirits of the east,*
> *powers of the flames rising in the morning.*
> *Hear my call—and be here with me!*

Call the south, raising your arm and facing that direction:

> *I summon and call upon the white spirits of the*
> *south, the final home of ancestral bones.*
> *Hear my call—and be here with me!*

Lastly, call the west. Raise your arm, facing this direction, and recite:

> *I summon and call upon the gray spirits of the west,*
> *powers of water over which the moon rises at dusk.*
> *Hear my call—and be here with me!*

Then, go to the center of your circle and recite the following declaration:

> *This circle is cast and bound.*

Now is a good time to evoke the Old Ones, allowing them to be present in your ritual and to lend their aid, guidance, and wisdom. These evocations can be found in Chapter Six, "The Old Ones and Other Spirits." If you are working with a particular spirit, call them now. Then proceed to whatever work you've got planned.

Going back to the description of where certain implements go in the Circle of Art, there is sacramental food and drink. These are consumed during the ritual, but you should leave enough to allow for an offering—a sip of the drink and portion of the food—to the Old Ones and spirits you are working with. The drink is traditionally wine, but an appropriate fruit juice makes for a good substitute if needed. The food is usually a type of grain, like bread or small baked goods. If you have multiple participants, make sure there is enough of the food and drink for everyone—plus an offering. When presenting each offering, take them from the west and south and present them to the north. Consume a portion of the food, and then raise the remainder to the north, reciting:

> *Ancient Ones, please accept this offering. As I partake, may*
> *I never hunger. Thank you for your guidance and wisdom.*

Then, consume some of the ritual drink. After doing so, hold the chalice to the north and recite:

> *Ancient Ones, please accept this offering. As I partake, may*
> *I never thirst. Thank you for your guidance and wisdom.*

Of course, all things come to an end—rituals too. To mark that, give final thanks and start in the north, bidding farewell to the elements and their domains until you meet next:

> *Black spirits of the north, powers of the spectral air, I thank*
> *you for warding and lending your power to this rite as it*
> *ends, and I bid you farewell to your castle in the north.*

Next, bid the west farewell; face that direction and recite:

> *Gray spirits of the west, powers of the deepest seas, I thank*
> *you for warding and lending your power to this rite as it*
> *ends, and I bid you farewell to your castle in the west.*

Then, head to the southern part of the circle and recite:

> *White spirits of the south, powers of the earth below,*
> *I thank you for warding and lending your power to this rite*
> *as it ends, and I bid you farewell to your castle in the south.*

Lastly, bid the east farewell, saying out loud:

> *Red spirits of the east, powers of the brightest flame,*
> *I thank you for warding and lending your power to this rite*
> *as it ends, andI bid you farewell to your castle in the east.*

Officially close the rite by treading about the space three times in the opposite direction from which you originally cast, then recite:

> *Just as I came in peace to this space, I depart in the same vein.*
> *May I go forth from here with wisdom, strength, power,*
> *and courage renewed. To the most ancient of beings, I ask*
> *that you protect, guide, and watch over me in the Old Ways.*
> *Until we meet again, this circle is unbound. So mote it be.*

Clear the space of any evidence that the working took place. Note that there are some exceptions to this, however. If you have a working that is going to take a few days to complete, feel free to leave it on a dedicated space where it won't be disturbed. For certain seasonal celebrations, leaving decorations and offerings about is acceptable to ring in the spirit of that season. Otherwise, put everything back in its rightful place and dispose of any remnants appropriately.

CHAPTER SIX

THE OLD ONES AND OTHER SPIRITS

In truth, the Old Ones are difficult to describe. There are many in number, face, and name; they take many forms. Yet, in this book, we will cover two overarching concepts of who the Old Ones are—dividing them into the masculine and feminine. To many traditional practitioners, the Old Ones are both deities and not simultaneously. They embody the natural forces of this world as well as the universe at large. These forces keep a balance all on their own, in their own time, on their own terms.

THE HORNED ONE

The idea of Witches worshipping a male horned deity equated with the Devil has been a recurring image in public consciousness for centuries, but the reality is that this version of the Devil was made by Christianity—the Horned Father in the Old Craft is quite different. He is largely an echo of the collective consciousness of early tribes that relied on hunting as a primary food source; thus, one of their primordial gods resembled the same horned animal that brought them life and nourishment. In fact, for some, the modern notion of the Devil serves more as an allegorical concept.

If we were to look deep into the history of Christianity in Europe and how most of the continent's Pagan population was converted (usually forced to by threat of death), we'd find that horned deities like the Greek Pan, Celtic Cernunnos, and Roman Ianus (or Janus) had been twisted into demonic figures. There is also evidence that this occurred with certain chthonic deities like Hades, or titans like Kronos and Saturn; even the Fae Folk in the British Isles were called "devils" in some Witch trials where the accused were thought to have mingled with them. This vilification was a conversion tactic used by Christian rulers to get their people to conform. It ensured that the people knew what their deities stood for in the eyes of this new religion—even though it was not much different from original Pagan associations.

The horned gods of Europe all had the following associations: The Wild Hunt, death, virility, freedom, knowledge, and the animalistic part of the human psyche. Additionally, the Horned Lord of the Craft has gone by many names in the lands he was recognized in: Janicot, Black Donald, Cernunnos, Pan, Ianus, Lucifer, Herne, and many others. Mainstream religions like Christianity preached control over this and other deities because religion became a way for rulers to control the masses. Rulers wanted morally upright people they could manipulate easily and who wouldn't question their leadership.

But even God can be viewed as an allegorical figure rather than a literal entity: the concept of perfection, morality, and striving to be our best selves. Being *closer to God* means being perfect, a feat that is unattainable for most people. In contrast, the Devil centers being human, meaning we are fallible and prone to making mistakes, as well as have needs for earthly pleasures that have become known as "sinful." We can see this same concept in Sigmund Freud's theory of the unconscious, where the human psyche is made up of what are known as the "id," the "ego," and the "superego." The id represents our fallibilities as humans, our shortcomings, and any urges we suppress in order for our ego (which is the *self*) to be healthily balanced (and so we don't get in trouble with authority figures).

The superego is the opposite, representing our highest good and what we strive to be. Putting this into perspective, the id can be compared to the Devil, while the superego can be compared to God. The ego—or self—is the person themselves, caught in between this profound dichotomy.

The story of Azazel, one of the many faces of the Horned One, being the original scapegoat is an interesting one to note. Azazel was a fallen angel and had a place in the atonement rites of Judaism. On Yom Kippur, Azazel was sent out into the desert to die and bear all the sins of the Jewish people. This was also one punishment he endured for teaching humans forbidden arts like sorcery, which was said to have corrupted humanity. To symbolize this, it was even customary at one time to drive a goat over a ravine to its death as a sacrifice for purging one's sins. Given that Azazel, for centuries, had been considered the Devil's wingman or the Devil himself, the goat has become synonymous with the Devil, aside from the existing horned deities in European folk religions. The idea of a horned entity being a scapegoat can be seen throughout history as people tried to blame their problems or wrongdoings on external factors, especially in times where they were expected to be pious. Thus, we get the phrase: *the devil made me do it.*

Aside from being an overall perversion of the old Pagan deity by the Church, the Devil may be represented as a horned animal, namely a goat, because the natural behaviors of this creature are symbolic of someone who does not follow the crowd. Goats are known to be highly independent. They do not flock together like sheep do. The latter of these may be the origin for the term *lamb of God;* likewise, people in large numbers who blindly follow an authority figure are sometimes called "sheep" or the slang word "sheeple," a blending of the words "sheep" and "people." Hypothetically speaking, if a goat were to see a flock of sheep in front of it, it would likely not follow their path for very long and instead go off to the side, on their very own path up the mountain.

A Call to the Horned One

Use this call when you wish to invite the Witch Father into your space—either for specific acts of magic or as a way to give him honor. If you feel called to compose your own, I encourage you to do so.

Great Horned One, master of the wild and free,
Hear my call!
Master of the fallen, keeper of knowledge hidden,
Hear my call!
Lord of life, death, and time,
I call to you with honor and respect.
He who bears the flame of enlightenment betwixt his horns,
He who presides over all earthly pleasures and revelries,
He who is King of the Sabbat and Lord of the Hunt,
Falling and rising and falling again,
He who holds the power of the winds and storms,
And the great serpentine fire in the earth's core,
He who is keeper and steward of the great green wild,
I call to you, I honor you.
Please be here, with me, in this hour.
Let it be known, your ancient power.

THE WITCH MOTHER

The feminine has always had a place in the Old Craft, and she takes many forms. The hag, the seductress, the healer, the weaver of fate's intricate web, she who cuts our umbilical cords at birth and the strings of life at death—the list goes on. Her skin glows like the moon, her semi-nude form adorned in the finest jewels, and atop her head sits a crown of stars symbolizing her station in the natural order. The Mother also appears veiled, her face obscured as she travels through the halls of the labyrinth. She is known to some as "the Queen of the Fae," residing in the world of Elphame beneath the trees. She has been known by many names, in many times, and in many lands—Hecate, Lilith, Diana, Nicnevin, Habondia, Hulda, Ereshkigal, Freyja, Aradia, Baba Yaga, Venus, Inanna, and so on.

It is no secret that with the rise of certain organized religions, any reverence of the feminine was forced to fall out of fashion in favor of patriarchal systems. Yet, even in religions like Christianity, some spark of it still existed through Mary, mother of Christ, and Mary Magdalene, the woman said to be his wife. The latter of these figures has been speculated to be anywhere from a prostitute to a priestess of a religion now considered long gone. Back in ancient Jerusalem, Mary Magdalene could have very well been a temple priestess where sacred sexuality played a huge part in the worship of a goddess. Such practices were also customary in Babylonia and Sumer, to such goddesses like Ishtar and Inanna. Temple priestesses who engaged in sacred sexuality were called "virgins," which simply meant that they were not under a man's authority, and instead had an obligation to the goddess they served. In times of war, soldiers came to the temples for worship—by engaging in religious fornication, the goddess worked her feminine power through these temple priestesses to heal and transform the soldiers from within, helping them cope with the physical and emotional wounds of war.

The womb is an important symbol of the Mother—both figuratively and literally. It is the start of all new things, so long as something is put into it. Historically, without the aid of modern technology, sperm had to enter the uterus and attach to an egg cell to conceive a child, which then attached to the uterine lining, finally developing into a baby. To grow crops, black soil had to be irrigated and plowed before seeds were put in it; when the crops were nurtured and able to become ripe, people and animals could survive. The womb is conceptualized as a dark, empty space—a receptive void of transformation.

Certain ritual tools in the Craft, like the cauldron, have this quality in order to manifest the will of the practitioner. You put something in the cauldron, and your will becomes manifest as it is born into reality by burning, boiling, mixing, and the like. It is a concept you use when working something brand-new with the qualities of something else. For example, if you write a petition to the spirits, it is merely the result of a union between paper and ink. If you burn said petition in your cauldron, the union of fire, paper, and ink is further melded into ash and smoke, which in turn sends your message to the unseen world. Using a mundane example, when you put ingredients together while following a recipe for chicken escarole soup, the end result is chicken escarole soup.

Another major theme associated with the Mother is that of fate. Numerous cultures have personified this concept as a triple deity like the Norns, or a singular goddess like Frigg, both hailing from northern Europe. In mundane life, such actions as spinning wool into yarn was considered magical. It was furthermore considered a woman's art, as women who could spin were women who could weave destiny. In the case of the Norns—or their Greek counterparts, the Moirai—they are said to spend eternity controlling the lives of all living things, especially humans. They do this by perpetually spinning the threads attached to them (which represent the courses of the lives of all creatures and the events within them) and cutting them loose when it is time for the person to die. The cultures that have goddesses like these often believe that fate and destiny are fixed, altogether unavoidable by humans. Interestingly enough, this idea of cords, fate, and women can be connected to the fact that babies are born attached to their mothers and their mothers' placentas by a cord.

Natural cycles are also a concept associated with the divine feminine. From this traditional perspective held by many ancient people, the cycles, such as menstruation, were attributed to the divine feminine and the experience of womanhood. This has long been connected to the moon, which is full once a month unless it is a blue moon, where there are two full moons in a month. Thus, a lot of lunar deities are depicted as female. Stories like that of Persephone's descent into the Underworld show that the divine feminine is also connected to the cyclical changes of the seasons. Persephone, the maiden daughter of the Greek harvest goddess Demeter, is abducted by the king of the dead, Hades, as he fell in love with her and wanted her as his bride. Some versions of the myth say that she went willingly to free herself from the control of her overprotective mother.

Demeter, in a state of despair, refused to tend to the fields that fed humankind. It became freezing cold, and snow began to fall. She went to Zeus for help, and he sent his messenger Hermes to retrieve Persephone. Hades was willing to give the maiden goddess back to her mother, realizing that life on Earth depended on it. However, to solidify their bond as husband and wife, he fed her a few pomegranate seeds first. Eating food from the Underworld meant that you were bound for life to it. When Persephone returned, this was discovered, and Hades compromised with the gods—she would spend six months above ground and be the herald of spring, but the other six months she would rule the Underworld with Hades as Queen of the Dead. With mythology like this, we can also see the duality that is present in some goddesses; Persephone was the goddess of spring and life, but also of winter and death.

If we take a look at mythologies and pantheons from around the world, we'll find that most (if not all) have some aspect of a goddess figure that rules over death and the underworld. In ancient times, the underworld was not necessarily a place of suffering or punishment. It simply was where bodies were buried: underneath the soil, which is associated with the feminine because growth happens in soil much like a baby grows in a womb. I generally refer to this idea as the "womb and tomb"; we come from the same place we go back to. We see this across many different mythologies the world over. One figure associated with this was the Mesopotamian goddess Ereshkigal, who became the queen of the underworld—or "Irkalla," as it was known after her brother Kur took her down there. The gods tried to rescue her, but she made do in her new home, as not even the gods could escape such a realm easily.

Ereshkigal also played a role in the classic myth of Inanna's descent. Inanna, the Queen of Heaven, was Ereshkigal's younger sister; one day, she ventured into the underworld with her servant. At each gate of the chthonic realm, Inanna was ordered to take off one piece of clothing until, when she finally got to the heart of the underworld, she was naked. When Inanna approached the throne where her sister sat, Ereshkigal was enraged by her hubris, killed her and hung her corpse from a hook on the wall. When the gods realized their beloved Queen of Heaven had been attacked, the world was turned upside down. Her father, Enki, sent down two demons. This threat worked, and Ereshikigal gave her sister's body over to them. Inanna was revived after being given nourishing food and drink, with the judgement of the Annunaki in her favor.[33]

Darkness is another traditional attribute of the feminine. Inanna having to undress in order to enter the underworld is a probable allegory for being totally vulnerable in a dark place, comforted only by the ability to reach into the deepest depths of your soul—much harder to conceal in the face of certain forces. Darkness has many allegorical and metaphorical representations, and these ideas can be applied to Witchcraft. For centuries, magical practices have been pushed into the darkness and considered "underground," a threat to establishments, or downright sinister. The darkness also represents the unknown. Witch or not, we all face the unknown and may even be afraid of it because when there is uncertainty, there is a lack of clarity on how to proceed or move on. Yet it is also in darkness that we plant the seeds which allow for our growth as people.

---

33 *Descent of Inanna.* University of North Carolina Wilmington, 2 Apr. 2009, people. uncw.edu/deagona/myth/descent%20of%20inanna.pdf.

The Mother also represents womanhood and the divine feminine in all life phases—youth, adulthood, and old age. In youth, she is a seductive, obscenely beautiful enchantress full of potential. In adulthood, she is a mother, a creatrix, a nurturer, and at her physical peak. As an elder, she is full of wisdom, self-aware, and a destructive energy given her proximity to death's door. An interesting thing is how Witches have been perceived over time—those various views seem to resemble how the Mother presents herself.

In many parts of the world, beautiful young women are said to be "bewitching" with their sexuality and charm, whereas their elderly counterparts were feared because of their perceived and earned wisdom, knowing so much that the establishment didn't. In life, womanhood is empowered by different strengths during different stages of life—some are left behind as aging runs its course, whereas others grow more distinguished for the remainder of a woman's days. In both cases, they contribute to the growth and empowerment of the divine feminine. Of course, you don't need to be a woman or have an experience of womanhood to be devoted to the Witch Mother; for example, I know many men who are and have developed beautiful practices from devotion to the Witch Mother.

A CALL TO THE MOTHER GODDESS

Use this call when you wish to invite the Witch Mother into your space—either for specific acts of magic or as a way to give her honor. If you feel called to compose your own, I encourage you to do so.

Ancient Mother, I call to you.
She whose womb is the void from which all things come,
She who presides over the cauldron of transformation,
She who cuts our cords from our mothers at birth,
And our souls from our bodies at death.
I call to you, I honor you.

Ancient Mother, ancestress of all Witches,
She who is the guardian of the vast and mighty seas,
And the fertile soil beneath our feet,
She who is both Queen of Heaven and of Hell,
She who spins the cords and weaves
the fabric of time and destiny,
I honor you, I call to you.
Please be here, with me, in this hour,
And make known your ancient power.

THE FAE FOLK

Also known as "fairies" or "the Good Neighbors," these nature spirits inhabit wild areas untouched by mankind. The lore of the Fae Folk comes from Europe, especially the Celtic diaspora, which spanned across the British Isles and parts of mainland Europe. Today, many of the most well-preserved myths about the Fae Folk come from the UK and Ireland. Italy is also known to have lore relating to the Fae Folk, with the goddess Diana being their queen. However, those across the Atlantic can still encounter them; perhaps some Fae Folk formed attachments to settlers from that part of the world and followed them to their new homes.

When Christianity came around, the view its leaders established as canon toward these creatures was that they were little devils or angels who had been thrown out of Heaven because they were not holy enough to be there, yet they were not evil enough to be down in Hell.[34] Thus, they stayed on Earth and developed domains in virgin forests and other natural places. In English and Scottish lore, the Fae Folk inhabited a realm called Elphame, meaning "elf home"

---

34   Oldridge, Darren. "Fairies and the Devil in Early Modern England." *The Seventeenth Century*, vol. 31, no. 1, Jan. 2016, pp. 1–15. doi:10.1080/0268117X.2016.1147977.

and considered the "city beneath the trees," as it was accessible by caves and hollows at the base of tree trunks via spirit flight. Their Queen was Nicnevin, or simply the Queen of Elphame. Even further back in Celtic mythology, the Queen was called Mabh or Maeve, who also was the goddess of ecstasy and inebriation. In Norse mythology, one of the Nine Realms is that of *Álfheimr*, ruled by the race of elves. It was split into two factions: one called "Ljósálfar," who were the white elves, and the subterranean dark elves called "Dökkálfar."[35] It is likely that Elphame of Scotland is a direct inspiration from Norse settlers or the result of the cultural mix that happened during the Viking raids.

The Fae Folk are not as sweet and adorable as the media like to portray them. They vary in appearance, looking like anything from goblins to animals to humanoids. They are known for playing tricks on humans, putting them in compromising or otherwise dangerous situations. In the olden days, they were as much feared as they were respected. To make one angry would almost certainly seal your fate. The Fae Folk were often blamed when things were lost or misplaced around the home; before science was the standard for explaining things, they were also blamed for disease and deformed children. It was believed they took human babies and replaced them with *changelings*, who had some kind of deformity or otherworldly quality that made others ostracize them as they grew up. It is important to acknowledge that like many beings, the Fae Folk do not share the same moral compass as humans, which is one reason why they were seen as evil or a nuisance. Making offerings to them as a means of keeping the peace is a wise move, but accepting gifts from them can have consequences that are dire to the mind and spirit.

Even though it is wise to keep the peace with the Fae Folk, it is also wise to maintain boundaries. A classic protective

---

35 "Elves in Norse Mythology." *Nordic Culture*, 24 Sept. 2020, skjalden.com/elves/.

measure against them is iron, a metal by which they are highly offended. Red berries, especially from holly, rowan, or mountain ash were considered to be apotropaic (or protective) as well. You're bound to notice when the Fae Folk are hanging around; if you are out in nature and feel like you are being watched, chances are that is the case. A physical manifestation of the Fae Folk are mushrooms on the ground, or fae plants like foxglove growing nearby. If you have ever seen a circular formation of mushrooms on the ground, this is called a "faerie ring." It is perilous to step into one, as it is a portal to their realm; you may lose time and sanity while you're trapped in it. Carry rosemary as a precaution when out in nature, and should you find yourself in a faerie ring, sprinkle it around and walk out, never turning back.

WAYS TO WORK WITH THE FAE

- Spend time in nature; the Fae Folk are *everywhere* in the natural world. The further away from civilization, the more likely you are to encounter them, but I have experienced them existing in places inhabited by humans. Make sure you are silent and listen to your surroundings.
- Leave offerings not just to keep the peace and as a means of protection, but also as a sign of respect for the land. I find that they particularly enjoy baked goods and sweets.
- Incorporate their presence in outdoor rituals. Just make sure you do not have any salt or tools made of metal (especially iron), as these are both highly offensive to the Fae Folk.
- Never force interactions with the Fae Folk. This will not end well, as they have minds of their own.
- If you own property, starting and maintaining a garden is a great way to interact not only with the Fae Folk but also the spirits of the land on which your house is built. You could even designate a section of your garden for the

Fae Folk, akin to an outdoor altar. Incorporate symbolism and decorations relating to them such as butterflies, mushrooms, toads, and even faerie lights. Plants you could cultivate that are rich in faerie lore are foxgloves, roses, and bluebells.

LAND SPIRITS

Land spirits are those that inhabit wild places and are native to them. The term comes from Roman mythology, where the *genus loci* were known as "spirits of place" that guarded said place. In modern times, it has evolved to describe the overall spirit, vibe, or atmosphere of a place. The Craft recognizes that most things have a spirit, not just living organisms. Stones, bodies of water, bones left behind by decay, even the tools we use—they all have an innate spirit. Thus, applying this to a place, there can be many in one. In modern cities, it can be difficult to give offerings or do work with them, but it is always nice to get out into the wilderness once in a while. If you are a city-dweller, you may want to take a drive out to the nearest nature reserve for a day-long excursion or a weekend retreat. You can even make this a vacation, though for Witches it can be a time to relax *and* develop a relationship with the Earth. Many practitioners in the olden days didn't travel far from home like so many of us do today, so keeping things local was a given even with their spirits. We are privileged to have advanced transportation that can take us to unique natural landmarks in hours or less.

In Northern Europe, the *landvættir* were spirits of place who could be as small as a stone or as large as a field. They are chthonic in nature, sometimes taking the form of the dead. This idea was brought over to England by the Saxons, and it is from here that we know them as "land wights."[36] Land wights

---

36 "What Are Wights?" Fyrnsidu, 17 Aug. 2021, fyrnsidu.faith/wights/.

are mentioned numerous times in the Norse sagas; one such work is the Egils saga, where Egil Skallagrimsson set up a cursing pole to agitate the *landvættir* enough to send away the king of Norway.[37] These types of spirits also appear on the Icelandic coat of arms. There are four in total: the bull, the giant, the eagle and the dragon.

In the Shinto religion of Japan, there is the concept of *kami,* which are divinities that personify forces of nature and elements of a landscape. Shinto beliefs explain the *kami* as being of nature, rather than apart from it; they possess both good and bad characteristics. In the West, this idea has been interpreted as being akin to that of land spirits or spirits of place.

Building relationships with land spirits can take a lot of time. It has taken me years to develop a relationship with local wild places, and it isn't without its dangers, mishaps, or inconveniences. I've been pricked by thorns and feasted on by hungry mosquitoes (even with adequate protection) before the time where said wild areas became calming places of repose and introspection. In the same vein, land spirits vary from place to place. The land spirits I knew in my late teens in one area are vastly different than the ones I've developed relationships with later on. In this respect, it's hard to take traditional practices from a place like Europe and replicate them because the *genus loci* of their lands are different than the ones on North American soil. For example, you may have a healing spell from the old country you want to attempt, but the land spirits near you are extremely different from what your ancestors may have encountered. However, this does not mean your attempt won't work at all—it just means you're facing different obstacles.

---

37 Green, W. C., translator. "Egil's Saga." Icelandic Saga Database, 1893, sagadb. org/egils_saga.en. Note: SagaDB is an online database of translations of the Icelandic sagas. Each saga is segmented into *kafli,* or chapters. Egil cursing the King of Norway can be found in Chapter Fifty-Eight.

In building a relationship with your local land spirits, offerings can and should be made. I personally recommend doing them at the base of trees you are drawn to; leave some sort of grain and wine. Water will also do if in doubt. Use your instincts and communicate with your local spirits to find out what is appropriate. Also, spending time in your landscape is a great way to develop a relationship with your local spirits. Listen to them, heed their warnings, hear their stories—there is so much to learn from them.

Ways to Work with the Land Spirits

- Get acquainted with the land on which you live. If you live in a small town, get to know the local history and folklore.
- Go out for walks in local nature. As I previously mentioned, the land spirits in my hometown were very different than the ones I met in the city where I went to university. Notice differences in the landscape; even plant species may be different. Take note of it all—should you go out on a foraging excursion, this knowledge will be especially helpful.
- Be aware that there are many types of land spirits—even the Fae Folk are considered land spirits. The same goes for people who lived, died, or were buried in this place.

Ancestors

Our ancestors were from many lands and times, spoke many tongues, experienced similar and different life events to us, had struggles and real emotions, and lived in unique cultures. We may not have hard artifacts from *all* of the people who ever existed, but we do carry a part of them every day—within our blood. In the Old Craft, the term *ancestry* can also refer to that of a spiritual nature, especially if you are in a tradition. In initiation, you become part of the spiritual lineage of the tradition in question; thus all initiates of the past become your spiritual ancestors.

Every year between October 31 and November 2, the high Sabbat of Samhaín takes place, also known as All Souls Day or All Hallows. In the Celtic calendar, these days mark the New Year. It is a time when the souls of the dearly departed walk freely among the living because the barrier between the worlds has faded. Participants pay homage to those who have gone before, and in my own experience, it is truly a time of year that brings you back to where it all started. I would say that the common notion of *the veil is at its thinnest* is erroneous and contradictory, because a veil in itself *is* thin, which means that the proverbial veil that separates the worlds of spirit and form is thin year-round. That said, you can technically honor your ancestors and work with them anytime, not just one night of the year. If anything, work with them as often as possible, as it is important to know where you come from and who your ancestors were.

If you were adopted or simply do not know much about your blood family, do some research. A DNA saliva kit can be a great start if you have no idea what your heritage makeup is. In a magical practice, this can be very useful because in theory, all of your ancestors live on through you, in your blood, and are always with you. You carry the blood of thousands in your veins. They each have skills and knowledge from which you can draw. For example, if your great-great-grandfather was a shoemaker, he more than likely knows how to run a business. If you are running a business in this modern age, his advice may be a bit dated, but some things hold true throughout time.

There are numerous ways to connect with your ancestors or beloved dead. You could keep a dedicated altar in your home with photographs and belongings of the deceased, where you can make offerings and commune with them. Even something like pouring yourself a drink and another in your chalice for the dead is a devotional act, sort of like you're having a drink with someone alive. It is very simple, but very effective and classic.

You can also get in touch with your ancestors by doing activities relevant to your culture or things that were once relevant in their lives. In my own life, I craft things by knitting or sewing, as my grandmothers did these activities while alive. I also have a passion for cooking, and around Christmastime, my mother and I make traditional Italian cookies to not only enjoy for ourselves, but to give as gifts to family and friends. When I was in high school and university, I had the chance to polish my Italian and French; even then, I knew it was a way to get in touch with my roots, knowing my maternal ancestors spoke the same languages.

What traditions or skills do you have in your family that you want to keep alive? Start there!

WAYS TO WORK WITH YOUR ANCESTORS

- Learn a skill that they had in life. Ask them to teach you how to be more proficient in said skill.
- Learn a language that they spoke and speak to them in said language. Do not stress if you can't get the pronunciations right. Keep in mind that the further you go back in your family tree, you may encounter languages that are considered extinct. So do not fret if you are of English ancestry and cannot find reliable sources on how to speak Old Saxon.
- Ask them to guide you in making important life decisions that affect your family.

THE DEPARTED

This chapter would not be complete without mentioning the dead. For millennia, in almost every culture, there has been lore about what happens to us when we die. Many believe that souls go to eternal bliss (heaven) or eternal damnation and suffering (hell). Others believe that we are reincarnated so that lessons can be learned between lives. There is a fraction of people who believe that this is our only existence and there is nothing in the here-after; still others believe in a purgatory-like state.

The truth is, *we really don't know,* collectively, what happens when we die. Yet, there are a lot of testimonies from people that can serve as answers to this question. A lot of them come from experiences with the dead. In the Old Craft, it is very possible to call up the spirits of the dead for either reverence or assistance with our work. This practice is called *necromancy;* as far back as the Middle Ages and the Renaissance, necromancy was *the* darkest art one could practice. It not only was a great interference with God's will, but it was greatly feared because like today, many people fear death and mortality. Despite its stigma, necromancy is not something a Witch should be afraid of, let alone death; we all get there someday. All things come to an end. Figuratively, necromancy is black magic because it is within black soil that we bury our dead—for their flesh to decay and their bones to rest.

The departed can be called up in a ritual setting or simply experienced in passing. They can also visit you in your dreams. This is especially true of loved ones who have passed over; they usually have a message to share or wish to bond with you. Personally, my ability to sense spirits increased greatly in my late teens. Not long after I came to the full realization of my strength in this area, I was able to feel presences passing by me in mundane places such as the train station. (This checks out, as a lot of stations are underground where the dead are buried.)

A practitioner of the Old Craft may call up the departed for aid in spellwork, to find out or learn information, or, if they are ancestors or beloved family members, for reverence in festivals such as All Hallows. When calling up someone deceased, be certain that you are setting boundaries with said spirit; do not allow them to enter your body without consent, and make sure you are able to banish them if things get out of hand. Have something connecting you to that spirit on hand, such as a personal belonging or photograph, as well as a reason *why* they are being called up. If there is a particular medium through which you want to receive messages, have that ready. I personally use automatic writing when communicating with spirits, but a pendulum may work if you are seeking *yes* or *no* answers.

If you are calling up the dead just for the fun of it, you may be putting yourself in serious danger. The dead are much like the living, except they no longer have bodies to occupy. They are like the living in the sense that they have personalities, likes, dislikes, and natural behaviors. Summoning any spirit without a purpose is like letting a stranger into your home—would you do that with someone alive? Didn't think so. Also, be sure to leave appropriate offerings for the spirit. You may need to do some digging to find out what a spirit enjoyed in life. You could also do this with ancestors or departed loved ones when honoring them in a ritual or if you seek to commune with them.

As you work, be aware of attachments. They can happen randomly, but they usually happen because you did not establish proper boundaries with the spirit you invoked. I have experienced spirit attachments a few times myself, and it took me a while to figure out that was what was happening. The first occurrence was when I was at a friend's birthday party. It took place at her mother's house, and everything was fine up until I went into the house to use the bathroom. To get there, I had to go through the kitchen, and I felt a very *off* vibe being there. I went, and then came back out. Just before having cake, I had this very clear sensation of being impaled from the back to the front, through my heart area. I was very intimidated by this and left the party, but not before giving my friend her gift. The whole experience took me aback, but it also made me realize there was some harmful residual energy in that house. I got home and tended to myself appropriately, but it didn't erase the fact that I was shaken up. The next time was when I was in university; this time, the source was initially unclear and it manifested as a single spot in the middle of my back. Nothing was physically there, but I felt a clinging sensation—I could physically move or wiggle about, and it would still be there. It took some divination to realize that this was a spirit attachment. This occurrence led me further into spirit work, because I knew I had to grow more proficient in order to deal with it. I did baths and spells, and before I knew it, the attachment was gone.

A few summers ago, at the time of writing this, there was a hate crime perpetrated in my hometown, resulting in two casualties. It shook everyone up, because a sleepy seaside community is the last place anyone would think this could happen. One of the victims (we will call them "G") found their way to me within two days of the incident. I felt their presence attach to my neck and back. I did not feel like they were doing me any harm, but I still felt the need to act. Rather than getting rid of the attachment like I had before, I decided to interact with the spirit and find out who they were, as well as what they needed from me. Everything was confirmed—no, this spirit was not going to hurt me. They were just lost, confused, and overall traumatized by their sudden, brutal end. After interacting with G, I was able to coax them off of me and direct them to where they needed to go first in order to get closure and healing. When G's body was laid to rest, that also helped remove the attachment.

Moral of the story: make sure you have adequate protection, even if you feel you don't need it. Also, if you feel a spirit is attached to you, trust your gut instincts. Get rid of it if you feel it's harmful; if you do not feel it will harm you, try to see what it wants or if you can intervene. Relationships with spirits of the dead are much like those with the living—they take work, time and effort. There is a give and take aspect to working with the deceased. Many practitioners, especially those new to the Craft, shy away from spirit work all together out of fear of being indebted to a spirit. It is normal to feel this way, but the reality is that sometimes an exchange needs to be made for an outcome to manifest. This is especially true if you are working a spell and utilizing a spirit's help. There is more on the ridding of spirit attachments in Chapter Eleven, "Practical Spellcraft."

Offerings

Offerings are customary when working with spirits and deities. The latter of these is more of a challenge because you'll want to ensure your deities are not offended by a certain offering. For example, it would be inappropriate to give mistletoe as an offering to Isis, considering it is not native to Egypt; but it *does* grow in Europe! Thus, I'd save the mistletoe offering for a deity like Odin or Thor. In the case of the Fae Folk, offerings can serve as a means of protection from their antics.

Here is a list of things that are considered universal offerings for most kinds of spirits. If you are unsure, go with your gut instincts or ask the spirit what they prefer. As previously stated, do the work of researching what a spirit enjoys, especially if they are dead and you wish to work with them. The list is as follows:

- Milk
- Honey
- Alcoholic beverages (wine, beer, mead, vodka, and so on)
- Baked goods
- Home-cooked meals
- Music
- Artwork
- Poetry
- Acts of service
- Fruits
- Fresh flowers
- Incense
- Oils (especially when anointing idols of deities)
- Lighting a candle
- Chanting and prayers

CHAPTER SEVEN

TO SEE, HEAR, FEEL, AND KNOW

People have always had a yearning to learn about their future love, money, health, and other general aspects of life, so those who have a knack for discerning such things are generally in high demand. Learning to develop your skills in the divinatory arts will prove valuable, not just to those who seek you out for council but also to your own Craft. I learned this firsthand as a professional psychic and tarot reader, having been asked many questions myself. Beyond being a side gig that I've really loved doing for some time now, such use of these extra-sensory abilities is one of the hallmark talents of the Old Craft.

Witches have always had a connection to the unseen since time immemorial. We can practice these abilities through divination methods or by themselves in their raw form. *Divination* is defined as the method of gaining insight into a question or situation by way of an occultic, standardized process. This is a collective practice with hundreds of methods that is not as exclusive to the Craft as people make it out to be; you don't even have to be a Witch to perform it. In fact, many diviners I know shudder at the very idea of being associated with Witchcraft, especially if they're used to traditional folk methods stemming from organized religion. In the Old Craft, though, having a keen sixth sense helps immensely for many reasons. For one, it can help you make decisions in everyday life. It can also help you predict the results of a working: the *how, who, when,* and *what* of the results. Doing so can help you precisely plan and execute a spell down to the finest details. Divining before a spell or ritual is extremely useful in determining if magic will be at all useful in a situation. It can also help you discern sincerity or folly in those around you. All in all, divination can help you change your life for the better. Keep in mind that extrasensory abilities are not extra senses in themselves. They go beyond that. They are merely extensions of what is already there. The ability to see, hear, smell, touch, and taste beyond physical means is a profound way to learn about the world around you, both seen and unseen. All extensions of the senses combine to form that *sixth* everyone is talking about.

Children are usually very sensitive to all things otherworldly; it is because of this that we can more easily tell if a child is to grow into following the ways of the Old Craft. A child may see the face of a deceased relative in a restaurant while the family is eating, but when they tell their mother what they saw, the mother will brush it off as mere imagination. Children also often play with *imaginary friends* that only they can see and interact with. If a child is showing more empathy than what is considered usual for someone of their age, especially toward non-human organisms like animals or trees, that is an early sign of them being empathic. A child who can remember past lives will speak in great detail of places and times in which they did not yet exist. Another sign of the onset of extrasensory talents in children is that of *dreaming true,* also known as "prophetic dreaming."

I have experienced many forms of psychic phenomena, all starting with prophetic dreaming at the age of twelve. Even before I started my path, I was having dreams about other kids from my classes and then seeing them in a store or doctor's office shortly thereafter. As I further practiced these skills, I felt led to make predictions with the old deck of playing cards my family used to use in games. One particular instance was when I predicted my seventh-grade teacher down to her name— when homeroom class assignments were posted the week before the year began, my name was listed under her classroom. My first pendulum was a pendant at the end of a lightweight chain, and I would scry with nothing but a bowl of water and a pink salt lamp as my light source. I also studied astrology much more in-depth than ever before, and I often tell people that astrology was my "first love." As years went by and I improved, I took my skills to social media and gave free card readings every so often, leaving many people satisfied by the answers I gave to their questions.

After my freshman year of college, I started to professionally read the tarot. I had many clients coming back one month after their initial reading for updates on their situations, as well as new clients by word of mouth. In my years of doing professional readings, I helped people from all over the world with various dilemmas in love, finances, career trajectories, and more. Even in daily life, there'd be incidents like one that occurred in a small occult shop a few cities away. I walked in to see not many people were in the store, and on a hunch, I said to the cashiers, "You guys are under new ownership." One of them, a man no older than thirty-five, asked me how I knew and that they had just signed the paperwork twenty minutes before I walked in the door. I chalked it up to a lucky guess, but he insisted that I was psychic.

One more anecdote I'll share is when I was first communicating with my former partner, in England at the time, before he went on a paranormal investigation in a castle. I tried my hand at determining the types of spirits he would come across, as this castle was very old and had seen many people pass in and out of it for five hundred years. Plus, paranormal investigation can be dangerous—he was very seasoned at it, but I was still pretty concerned. The following day, he sent me a message confirming that the types of spirits I saw in my divination were the types he encountered in the castle during his investigation. So I—four thousand miles away in the US—had been able to discern this information about a castle in England I had no prior knowledge of. It is indeed possible.

However, developing psychically as someone born with such abilities is not a walk in the park. As I experienced personal traumas and even certain deaths or losses in my life, they only grew stronger; there were times where I didn't know if I could handle it. One example: for years I suppressed my natural talent for communicating with spirits, mainly because of my conditioning, or it could have been because I did not feel ready to be fully surrounded by that part of existence just yet. When I was in my late teens, I started to see white mists in the air with the naked eye, when there was *no* misty or rainy weather. It was something that truly shocked me. This also happened intermittently as I ventured into wooded areas, hiked rocky terrain, and looked out at the treetops down below. In moments like that, you truly get to know the spirit of the place you are hanging around in.

Without further ado, here are the *clairs*, a category of well-known abilities in relation to the five natural senses:

- **Clairvoyance:** extrasensory seeing
- **Clairsentience:** extrasensory touch or feeling
- **Clairaudience:** extrasensory hearing
- **Clairolfactus:** extrasensory smelling
- **Clairgustance:** extrasensory taste

This is not a finite list, however—there are actually a bunch of different psychic abilities one can have, some of which may fall under one of the *clairs*. The ability to see auras is very well-known; it allows one to perceive the electromagnetic field around an organism and, sometimes, objects. This field usually manifests as one or multiple colors—and is indicative of the spiritual frequency of the subject. In some forms of alternative medicine, the aura also indicates the health of a living thing. Another phenomenon is that of astral projection, the ability to leave one's body and travel on the physical plane as well as the many planes of existence. OBEs (out of body experiences) fall under this category; in fact, many people experience this at least once in their lives while in deep sleep. Historically, Witches were thought to fly because they used certain ointments to make them astral project and affect the world around them. Go to Chapter Ten, "Oneiric Ventures," for more on this phenomenon.

Another well-known ability in the world today is that of empathy. Empathy is the capacity not just to sympathize with but also deeply understand what someone else is going through. In the psychic sense of the word, this is the ability to feel others' emotions and feelings as if they were your own. It can also encompass physical sensations, such as feeling pains in your own body when someone around you has an actual injury in that area of their body. In my own experience, empathy is the hardest to deal with and control. If you're empathic, everything you feel, you feel deeply to your core and then deeper. This is why many empaths shut themselves off emotionally and seem like cold, unfeeling people, when in reality, it is a defense mechanism for self-preservation. Many who possess this gift resort to substances to drown out any deep feelings they harbor. This is not a healthy way to deal with your emotions, and it is important to keep a reign on them as much as you humanly can. Without careful moderation, spiritual empathy can overtake and destroy the person in question.

Prophetic dreaming, also known as "dreaming true," is defined as dreaming of future events *or* of things that can be divined in relation to future events. Prophetic dreams can be interpreted like most other dreams, yet I find that this specific type of dream often depicts an entity making itself known to you through something it's shown you. This goes hand in hand with dream interpretation, a form of divination. Aside from the empirical skill of creating tests and assessments for research or diagnostic purposes, psychometry is also the term for a divinatory ability to feel or gather information from objects by touching them. Certain psychic abilities specifically zoom in on a period of time; for example, precognition helps one gather intel on future events and, subsequently, take a course of action to further cause or prevent something from happening, whereas retrocognition deals with past events.

DEVELOPING YOUR DIVINATION SKILLS

The key to developing psychic talents is to have a mind and body that is strong and sound. In my experience, having a healthy body—as well as generally feeling well-rested and nourished—makes a huge difference when divining for yourself or someone else. It also goes a long way in developing your psychic abilities. Some great herbs that help develop skills in this department include mugwort, wormwood, eyebright, and poppies. A great starting exercise for perception is what I call *sensory expansion;* I have taught it to some of my students, and they have found it very helpful. It works best when you are totally calm and in a quiet, peaceful setting. Sit comfortably, either outside in nature or in a calm room in your house. Take a few deep breaths, relax your muscles. Close your eyes— and start by focusing on your sense of smell.

As you inhale, what do you smell in your surroundings? Flowers, trees, grass, fresh earth? Maybe it's that air freshener plug-in, or the lingering sweetness of blueberry pancakes you had for breakfast? Either way, make mental notes as you take in all of the aromas around you. Your sense of taste comes next; unless you're eating, all you may be tasting in that moment is your breath, or maybe the aftertaste of your lunch. Either way, make note of it—it counts. As for your sense of touch, what do you feel around you? Is it the clothes clinging to your skin? The breeze blowing through the trees above? Do you feel like someone or something might be there? Keep your eyes closed and feel with your body, staying still. Let whatever presents itself do so in its own time. Now, it's time to expand your sense of hearing. Going off all of the other stuff you did, what can you hear? Do you hear birds above you? Are those the footsteps of a distant hiker? Do you hear running water from a creek not too far from where you are? Again, make note of what your ears perceive. You can even visualize a field around your head with this one, expanding slowly; the more it grows, the more you can hear. Lastly, your eyes. Open them slowly. What can you see before you?

Is the lighting or are the colors of things around you any different? Is there anything you see now that you did not see before you closed your eyes? Following this exercise, you may find changes in your overall perception—if it is done on a consistent basis. You may even find certain senses to be sharper than others. From here, you can determine which of the five *clairs* you possess.

DIVINATION METHODS

As mentioned, divination methods are numerous and come from cultures the world over. They are often paired with extrasensory abilities, except they employ standardized processes in order to get results. For example, in many forms of cartomancy, each card means something. I would definitely say that cartomancy and extrasensory abilities are independent of each other, but they tend to be used together. When I am reading tarot for clients, I pair the meanings of the cards drawn with my natural extrasensory talents in order to relay any messages to my client. However, there are also moments in private sessions where I do not have to draw any cards at all, and things within my client's situation come about how I perceive them.

The following list of methods—and some background to go with them—should cover the majority that are used in the world today:

ASTROLOGY

One of the oldest forms of divination, astrology has been in use for thousands of years across many cultures; thus, many systems have developed. It involves the analysis of the alignment of cosmic bodies such as stars and planets in our known solar system during a particular frame of time. The most common systems are Western, Eastern Sidereal, Vedic (Indian), and Chinese.

Astrology uses no—if very little—extrasensory talents at all. This ancient art is more about knowing how the stars and planets move about in the sky, for how long, and how to accurately place them where they belong on a diagram called an "astrological chart." This shows the alignments and relationships between planets, signs, and stars on a given date and time. Thus, true astrology is different than newspaper horoscopes or astrology apps—those are usually products of creative writing with no substance save for vague information based on the common qualities of the signs. They tend to be different depending on the sources you look at, as well as cryptically written in order to appeal to a bunch of people at the same time.

Simply put, charting astrological alignments or aspects involves planets in between and in relation to each other via a degree system. Each sign is categorized by the four classical elements and modalities, which are mutable, cardinal, and fixed. *Major aspects* include conjunctions, sextiles, squares, trines, and oppositions. Each body is charted in a sign at a particular point in time; for example, if you were born on February 1, your Sun would be charted in Aquarius—that is your Sun sign, said to represent your personality. Your Moon sign represents your psychology and emotions, that which you keep hidden. Your Ascendant shows how you present to other people around you. These alignments are commonly called the "Big Three." After this are the other planets and their meanings. Some charts go in-depth about asteroids in our solar system. That is about as in-depth as we will get here, as this is not an astrology book. There are numerous resources out there at your disposal should you find yourself drawn to this ancient art. One such resource I have used time and time again is the website Café Astrology, which has the capability of running all kinds of astrological reports, including natal charts.

CARTOMANCY

This is otherwise known as "divination by cards." Classically, these were playing cards or tarot, but today we have oracle and angel cards on the market for the tamest of tastes. Cartomancy is said to have originated in ninth century China, but the cartomancy we know today may have come from Persia in the form of circular *ganjifa* cards.[38] The tarot is another type of card commonly used for divination, but that was not their original purpose. Originating from fifteenth century Italy, they were inspired by playing cards brought through trade with Egypt.[39] The monarchs and nobles wanted decks much like those brought over, and they commissioned artists to create custom cards and decks for their families. Thus, the tarot was born. The oldest known tarot decks are the *Solabusca* and *Visconti-Sforza;* they were mostly used for games and entertainment. In the eighteenth century, however, things changed—cartomancy began being practiced with the tarot, and they've been associated ever since.[40]

In the nineteenth century, with Western occultism becoming popular, the *Rider-Waite* deck was created, and to this day, it is the most well-known tarot deck in the entire world. A tarot deck typically has seventy-eight cards, unless you own a specialty deck with more or less cards. Other styles of decks used for cartomancy also exist, like that of the French Lenormand and German Kipper cards. The former of these originated in nineteenth century Paris and are a series of thirty-six picture cards. They are named after Marie Anne Lenormand, a fortune-teller and personal advisor to numerous figures at the time, such as French Empress Joséphine de Beauharnais and Russia's Tsar Alexander II.[41] Kipper cards, which were first published in

---

38 Cal, Frances. "Persian and Indian Playing Cards." *Eastern Art at the Ashmolean Museum,* 2 Nov. 2017, blogs.ashmolean.org/easternart/2017/11/02/persian-and-indian-playing-cards/.

39 Parlett, David. "Tarot | Playing Card." *Encyclopedia Britannica,* 7 Apr. 2009, britannica.com/topic/tarot.

40 Revak, James W. "Biography of Etteilla / Great Tarotists of the Past." Villarevak.org, 2001, villarevak.org/bio/etteilla_1.html.

41 Delistraty, Cody. "The Surprising Historical Significance of Fortune-Telling." *JSTOR Daily,* 26 Oct. 2016, daily.jstor.org/surprising-historical-significance-fortune-telling/.

Germany in 1890,[42] have more mysterious origins; they are also composed of thirty-six picture cards. One primary difference cited between these two oracle-style decks is that Kipper cards are more capable of predicting larger-scale events.

SAMPLE READING SPREADS

Cartomancy is typically employed by way of spreads, in which cards are arranged in a certain way to represent an aspect of a situation or a question being asked. The proximity of a card to another—in addition to reversed or upright placements—helps to interpret a spread. There are thousands of spreads, and many practitioners even come up with their very own. Some use the tried-and-true and find it gets the job done. If you are just starting cartomancy, I highly recommend getting acquainted with your new deck. I like to sit with the deck—my mind clear and free of worries—and look at the depictions of figures and symbolism on them. Make note of anything that sticks out to you, even the imagery of the archetypes that decorate the tarot.

Whenever someone asks me how to start with spreads, I always recommend what's called a "single-card pull." This tactic doesn't just give you another means of getting to know your deck, but it's also a perfect start for actually reading the cards. When I first started my cartomancy journey, I kept a journal dedicated to any readings I did, even single-card pulls. I recommend incorporating this into your morning routine. When you pull a card, use your instincts to allow it to tell you a story. Let its imagery speak to you and allow you to make predictions in the day ahead. Write down what you think will happen in the day based on the card you pulled; that way, you can look back and reflect on your perceptions at the time of the pull.

---

42 "Information about Kipper Cards." The Fortune Tellers Society, 1 Dec. 2017, thefortunetellerssociety.com/information-about-kipper-cards/.

In my personal journey, I eventually decided to challenge myself with other spreads. One that I credit for helping me make predictions as well as I do is *a spread for the week ahead*. This spread incorporates seven cards, representing the days of the week from Sunday to Saturday, surrounding a center eighth card which represents the overall influences of the week.

A spread that looks identical to the week ahead is that of the *diamond*, but the difference is that the diamond is used to explain influences around a person or situation. You can easily turn this into a spread with fourteen cards, pulling a clarifier for each one in the diamond to gather even more precise detail.

Another great spread for beginners is the versatile *three-card spread*. This triad of cards can represent a variety of things, such as past-present-future, mind-body-spirit, problem-advice-solution, and so forth. When I do a three-card spread, I usually add a fourth card to clarify all the cards and provide an explanation of the spread's overall influences.

A classic spread in the tarot world is that of the *Celtic Cross*. This is a ten-card spread that is extremely adaptable and provides even more detail than the previous few spreads I mentioned.

There is a shorter version of this, the *Cross*, and it is exactly as it sounds: a six-card spread in the shape of a cross. This diminutive version of the previous spread can be used for simpler questions that a Celtic Cross would be too much for.

A *pyramid* spread is amazing to use when predicting timelines, ultimate goals, or the outcomes of plans. It is ideal for creating strategies. You can use as many tiers as you want, but three or four is a good start. The pyramid style is read from the bottom (the widest part) to the top (a single card).

A *tableau* is a type of spread that is grid-shaped, and the proximity of each card to the others is paramount to a successful reading. While popular with use of the Lenormand deck, it can be adapted to any deck you have. I usually do tableaus with up to sixteen cards at a time. This method of reading is excellent for complex situations needing deep analysis and insight.

CHIROMANCY

This is divination by analysis of the hands, especially the methods used in *palmistry*. On a hand, such features as bumps, lines, finger lengths, or even bone structure are analyzed not so much for divining the future, but for assessing the personality of whom the hand belongs to. Thus, this is a learned skill; you do not need to have heightened extrasensory abilities to perform it. Historically speaking, the true origin of chiromancy is unknown, but it is thought to have come from China or India and then spread into the West from there. However, this art may have been practiced as far back as Mesopotamia. In the Renaissance, chiromancy was on a list called the Artes Prohibitae, acts deemed to be direct transgressions against the canon law of the Catholic Church. This list also included necromancy.[43] In recent centuries, it has been associated with the nomadic Romani people, who travel from place to place with fortune-telling as their livelihood.

COMMON PALMISTRY SYMBOLS

Palm-reading is just what it sounds like: the lines on a palm are read. Some practitioners even take the hand shape into account; I have personally seen this consideration paired with categorization by the classical elements. Earth hands have square palms, short fingers, and often a rougher texture. Air hands have long, tapering fingers and square palms with skin soft to the touch—almost like touching a feather. Fire hands have shorter fingers and long palms. Water hands are described as having proportionately long palms and fingers. The most referenced lines in palmistry are the head, heart, and lifeline. There is also a fate line, which is ambiguous because not many people have it. Other distinctive markings on the hand have

---

43 Heiduk, Matthias, Klaus Herbers, Hans-Christian Lehner, Walter de Gruyter, eds. *Prognostication in the Medieval World: A Handbook*. De Gruyter, 2020.

been associated with psychic powers or healing capabilities. Chiromancy is a popular form of divination, but it does not foretell the future of the person whose palm is being read; rather, it showcases their personality. Palm lines and the shape of the hand can also change over a period of years.

RUNES

Runes are ancient alphabets typically written on stones or fragments of wood. Their origins can be traced back to third-century Denmark and Northern Germany. By the fifth century, runes known as "the futhark" spread to Scandinavia and parts of the modern-day Netherlands. They were commonly known as the "Elder Futhark." After this, various forms of it appeared throughout the Germanic diaspora. By the Viking Age, there were several forms of the futhark used within the parts of Europe they settled. By the ninth century, the Younger Futhark was very common; in fact, across Scandinavia, about six thousand inscriptions on large bedrocks survive to this day. Most, though, stand in Uppsala in Sweden and serve as memorials to the dead.[44]

Aside from divination, runes have an important role in the traditional magical practices of Northern Europe. Depending on what kind you are using, they are divided into *aettir* (singular: *aett*), each one named after a deity in the Norse pantheon. One is named for Freyja, the goddess of love, sexuality, beauty, war, and magic. Another is named for Heimdall, the watchman of the gods. The third is named for the war and law deity, Tyr.

Runes are traditionally read by being cast onto a flat surface. If you have a set, shake them up in your bag, thinking about what you wish to know. Then, pour the bag out onto said flat surface. Keep any that are laying face up, and put any that are face down back into the bag. Interpret from there, making note of the runes that are facing up. Notice where and how they fall,

44   Harrison, Dick and Kristina Svensson. *Vikingaliv.* Natur och kultur, 2007.

as well. A rune's proximity to another rune has meaning, as does whether the runes have fallen closer to you on the table or further away. The latter is indicative of time. The closer a rune is to you, the nearer in the future something will happen. Take this example; you cast out runes and the closest ones to you are Gebo and Othila. This foretells generosity from your family or ancestors. If runes fall further away from you on the surface, that means the interpretation applies to something further in the future. Let's go back to our example; you have Gebo and Othila nearest to you, but further away you see Thurisaz and Kenaz have fallen right next to each other, an omen of misfortune and disaster. Then, maybe halfway between these runes, you see a combination of Perthro, Mannaz, and Algiz in formation. This signifies a man and a sense of protection, but it is unclear from there; Perthro is the rune of the unknown and the secret. Why is this man coming forth? Where is this protection coming from? Is it from the man? You may not know right then. In this example, it would be wise to maintain prudence and caution in order to avoid any chances of disaster striking.

SCRYING

This is the ancient art of gazing into a reflective surface to receive visions with the naked eye. It can be done with a crystal ball, a black mirror, or even water. The idea is to focus on one point in the reflective surface until you become entranced enough to see shapes forming. These shapes then become visions, which should be relevant to you or the person you are scrying for. Compared to the other forms of divination on this list, successful scrying does require some level of extrasensory ability. Results of this can be anything from symbols to elaborate visions. You may see the faces of beings both physical and unearthly, as well as places both physical and not. If you want to get an idea of how to scry, the following procedure specifically details how to do so with a crystal ball and a black mirror. This method can also be employed with a simple bowl of water in a dark area.

Before using a crystal ball or a black mirror to scry, make sure it is properly dedicated for your purpose. First, create a wash solution with the following herbs: two pinches each of mugwort, wormwood, and eyebright, all of which are associated with psychic enhancement and sight. Your base can be water, but it is better to use high-proof vodka. As you craft the wash, visualize its purpose. Let it steep before you start to cleanse the crystal ball or black mirror. Dampen a cloth with the solution you made, and as you cleanse the surface, say:

> *By the spirits of these all-seeing plants and the waters of cleansing, you are clean and clear of any impure energies.*

Pass the mirror or crystal ball over some cleansing incense and say:

> *By this smoke, you are cleansed and repurposed. May all foreign energies escape this vessel and into the ether, banished from here.*

Now, breathe life into your scrying tool of choice; it is then ready to use. When not in use, store this object away in a dark area that the sun will not touch. However, like most dedicated tools, it is best to use it as soon as possible.

Ready to scry? In order to start the process, make sure the environment is set up for it. Burn an incense associated with psychic enhancement or clear sight such as myrrh, damiana, acacia, dittany of Crete, wormwood, mugwort, or eyebright. Ensure the room is entirely dark, save for the light of a few candles. I prefer to have them in a triangular formation around the device I am using, but they have to be far enough away to cast a faint light in its reflection. Once the incense is burning and the candles are lit, go into yourself. Close your eyes and decide on a question to ask. If you're scrying to get in touch with a particular spirit, invite them to join you. When you've decided on a question and have centered yourself, open your eyes and speak to the mirror or crystal ball. Say:

> *Vessel of clarity and sight, window into the other*
> *realms, aid me in finding the answers I seek.*

If trying to contact and communicate with a spirit, say:

> *Vessel of clarity and sight, window into the other realms, aid*
> *me in contacting and communing with the spirit of (name).*

If the spirit is that of someone who has passed on, having something around that once belonged to them can help immensely in bringing them forth. It is also helpful to write down what you see. If your aim is divinatory in seeking answers to a question, you may see vague symbols that relate to the answer. The process may involve putting two and two together a bunch of times, but an answer can be formulated.

When done, close the session by waving your right hand over the crystal ball or black mirror, saying:

> *Window to the spirit world, I thank you for*
> *your aid. I also bid thanks and farewell to any*
> *and all spirits of help to me on this night.*

As with any other working, leaving offerings such as wine or lighting more incense are great ways to pay homage to those who have helped you.

PENDULUM

A rather simple method of divination involves a pendulum, which is a small weight hanging from a length of cord so that it can swing freely, either back and forth or in (counter) clockwise circles. It is an ideal and quick way to find answers to *yes* or no questions, and for those who practice dowsing, this is also a useful tool. One method in determining the answers to questions is that if it swings back and forth, the answer is *yes*, much like a nod. If it swings left to right, the answer is *no*, much like someone shaking their head. If you are basing your interpretations on the pendulum swinging in circles, clockwise would mean *yes* and counterclockwise would mean *no*. Pendulum divination has also been used to predict the gender of a baby. In Italy, it is traditionally done by tying a wedding ring to a ribbon and holding it above the pregnant woman's abdomen. If the ring swung in a circle, it is a baby girl. If it swung back and forth in a straight line, it is a baby boy.

TASSEOMANCY

This is a popular method of divination, done with tea leaves, coffee grounds, wine sediments, or other residues, usually from beverages. The idea is related to scrying, except it is more tangible and open to interpretation because when the wet tea leaves stick to the inside of the cup, they form shapes. Special teacups for this purpose are sold with the inside separated into sections—for example, one section for love, one for career trajectories, and so on. This form of divination can be traced back to the Mediterranean regions, especially Greece and Turkey.

FINAL THOUGHTS

Do not be discouraged if you find yourself having a hard time with divination methods or the development of your extrasensory talents. Yes, it is true that you can inherit extrasensory talents from your ancestors, but never forget that all humans have some form of intuition off which they can develop these talents if dedicated enough. After all, our instincts have helped us survive as a species for millennia. Sometimes, you try things, and they aren't for you. I can remember first starting to explore different divination methods, and while I found my footing in things like carto-mancy and scrying, I did not do so with chiromancy or tasse-omancy. It may be the same for you—that is perfectly okay. As humans and practitioners, we are all unique and have our own strengths; finding where your proficiencies lie may take time, but it's all worth it in the end.

CHAPTER EIGHT

FAMILIAR SPIRITS

A classic association Witches have is that of the familiar. This has often been depicted as an animal in service to the Witch and their practice, but folklore suggests otherwise. The *familiar spirit* is not your pet cat; in fact, it is not corporeal at all. It is a spirit that is in service to you; in other words, you develop a working relationship with it. You can have multiple familiar spirits, and they all can be referred to by name. Sometimes, familiar spirits do not so much resemble animals as they do humanoid creatures or imps—or even hybrids of different beings. They truly have lives—and minds—of their own.

Throughout various Witch trials in Europe, there have been claims of familiar spirits being the otherworldly companions of Witches. In the old lore, familiar spirits were gifts from the Devil, ruler of all wild beings and places. Various accused people spoke of their familiars in their confessions. In 1646, Elizabeth Chandler of Huntingdonshire insisted she had difficulty controlling her familiar spirits, affectionately called Tullibub and Beelzebub.[45] A Witch from Wiltshire named Anne Bodenham confessed that she called her familiars by

---

45 Davenport, John. "The Witches of Huntingdon, Their Examinations and Confessions; Exactly Taken by His Majesties Justices of Peace for that County." Early English Books, 1646, quod.lib.umich.edu/cgi/t/text/text-idx?c=eebo2;idno=A81978.0001.001.

reading—something unheard of for most people in 1653.[46] In Scotland in 1662, Isobel Gowdie mentioned the names of familiars and other Witches in her coven to her interrogators, and even claimed the ability to shapeshift into a hare.[47] Meanwhile, thirty years later in Salem, Massachusetts, Sarah Good was described as having a familiar who took on the form of a yellow bird and suckled blood from between her fingers.[48] It was widely believed that a Witch's power diminished if her familiar was killed. This led to many cats and similar animals being killed out of pure fear that somewhere, they each had a Witch to serve.

One commonality with familiar spirits is that they *live betwixt*, taking the form of a creature who inhabits a combination of air, land, or sea. This is especially true if the familiar spirit resembles an earthly animal. The term *betwixt* refers to the concept of such beings moving between worlds. Interestingly, this is one of the natures of a Witch, for a Witch is a living vessel in between all dichotomies. Toads—creatures long associated with Witches—make great familiars because they occupy water and land as an amphibian. Crows inhabit both air and land, given that they fly and perch. Snakes are another great example of a familiar, as they slither around over (or under) the soil, and some species are aquatic. Animals that occupy all three of these realms in nature also make fantastic familiars, such as geese or ducks. In some traditions of the Old Craft, a familiar can take the form of a plant, serving as an ally to your workings. There have even been accounts in history where the spirit of someone long deceased became a familiar spirit, such as the

46 Notestein, Wallace. *A History of Witchcraft in England from 1558 to 1718*. Gutenberg, 2010.

47 Davies, Melissa. "Isobel Gowdie - Witch of Auldearn." Discover the Highlands and Islands of Scotland, discoverhighlandsandislands.scot/en/story/isobel-gowdie-witch-of-auldearn.

48 "SWP No. 063: Sarah Good Executed July 19, 1692." Salem Witch Trials Documentary Archive, salem.lib.virginia.edu/n63.html.

case of accused Scottish Witch Bessie Dunlop. During her confessions, she told authorities that one of her familiars was the spirit of a slain officer who had died three decades before, named Thomas Reid.[49] Though she was known as a healer in her hamlet, it is said she predicted people's deaths—such as that of her husband and child—with Thomas's help.

Familiars are capable of all sorts of things—they protect, they guide, they serve as messengers—and if you have multiple familiars, they tend to have different functions. You may have a familiar who resembles a creature small enough to fit into tiny spaces, which thus can travel to where you physically cannot. You may have a familiar spirit that flies in order to send messages or influences to where you need them sent. Another example is having a familiar that is so spiritually menacing that it will, in some mysterious way, cause grave harm to an enemy if they so much as think of hurting you. Familiars may also have specialized skills. If your familiar takes the form of an animal whose defense is to run away from danger, you can use that to your advantage by embodying said familiar to help you evade danger in a particular situation. A plant familiar can assist you with connecting to the green world, teaching you of the many cures and poisons that lie outside your backdoor. Such familiars often manifest as plant spirits that you have a deep connection with, be they a tree, an herb, a flower, or a bush. Once your familiar is attained and reveals its name to you, *never* under any circumstances give its name to anyone else, regardless of if they are a practitioner or not. There is power in a name, and with familiars, it is no different. Only *you* have power over your familiars, and by giving up their names, you're giving that power to someone else who could decide to steal them—or, worse yet, use them against you.

How does one get a familiar? Can you choose what it is? Traditionally, you cannot choose what form your familiar takes.

---

49 Love, Dane. *Legendary Ayrshire: Custom, Folklore, Tradition.* Carn Publishing Limited, 2009.

That is bestowed upon you by the folk Devil. A common way to determine what form your familiar will take is by observing the animals that make appearances in your life; or, it could be an animal you have been drawn to since you were a young child. You can perform rituals, like the one below, to call your familiar to you if you do not presently have one. However, it is not uncommon for you to have one while being unaware of its astral existence; in such case, the following ritual can also help acquaint you with your familiar.

CALLING YOUR FAMILIAR

Pick a quiet evening where you will not be disturbed. Light a black candle (this color being associated with the spirit world) from which your familiar is to come. Burn patchouli incense. Gaze into the flame, to the point where you feel your eyes starting to get heavy, and then close them. For the space of nine heart-beats, hold in your mind that which you wish to summon— your familiar. Say three times with conviction and will:

From the dark winds of spirit hailing from the North,
I call upon my spectral companion; be here, come forth.

Let your mind wander into a light trance, your eyes closed. Become receptive to the visions you receive as the smoke rises into the ether. Feel your mind drifting off into a clearing before dense woods; in front of you lies a narrow trail into the wilderness. Project your consciousness into this journey, and keep your senses aware. If you hear a particular sound in this vision quest, pay attention to where it is coming from. Most of all, keep your astral eyes peeled, as the first crea-ture you see and feel a pull towards is likely your familiar. Reach for it, almost as if you can touch it. Let the creature get a feel for you, as well. It may choose to reveal its name, but don't be in such a rush if this is your initial contact. It is highly probable that a familiar will show itself to you in dreams first. If you do not succeed in the vision quest, try again the following night. If still not successful, it may not be the appropriate time for you to establish contact with the familiar. Don't despair—you'll get there.

Maintaining and Bonding

After you have established a relationship with your familiar, you may see signs and shapes of them everywhere, even in the most unique of places. You may see that animal in everyday life in a corporeal form. For example, if your familiar takes the form of a rabbit, you may see more rabbits around than ever before out in nature. Keep in mind: your relationships with your familiars are no different than earthly ones, in the sense that you have to work to maintain them.

Old lore states that Witches fed their familiars blood, either through drawing their own blood or through a hidden nipple on their body.[50] However, as a modern traditional practitioner, I advise *against* feeding your familiar spirit blood, especially if your familiar takes the form of an herbivorous animal. It makes no sense to feed a corporeal herbivore blood or meat, so why should the non-corporeal version be any different? Plus, remember what was written earlier about familiars having minds of their own? Your blood is your life force in its purest form; your familiars could take it and run with it if they became displeased with you, and that would spell utter disaster. It's best to avoid all of that—after all, there are many other offerings you can give your familiar. Milk, oats, or even plain water are all considered acceptable.

A great way to bond with your familiar spirit, especially if it takes the form of an earthly animal, is to obtain parts

---

50 Murray, Margaret Alice. *The Witch-Cult in Western Europe.* 1921.

of that animal for personal use. I'm not saying to go out and kill an animal just for this purpose—there are many places you can ethically obtain such parts as furs, feathers, teeth, skulls, and more. In a city about thirty minutes away from my hometown, I went into an occult supply store that had animal bones, feathers, and furs as part of their offerings, and happened upon a pelt that was the exact same color as my familiar's in the astral plane. From there, I began strengthening my relationship with it by simply going into a trance state and stroking the fur as though the creature were alive, breathing, and able to respond. You may feel silly doing this, let alone speaking to your familiar while doing this, but it's a great way to sympathetically bond with your familiar. If for some reason you cannot get a hold of a cat's claw or deer antlers, a statue or figurine can serve as a representation of your familiar.

While work involving familiars can be used for a variety of purposes, I am including a few simple ones here which you can try on your own. It is worth noting that the stronger the relationship you have with your familiar spirit(s), the better the results will be.

If you have a familiar spirit that can fly, you can use this characteristic to send messages across a long distance to someone. Make sure that the person you are sending a message to is asleep; this is a very vulnerable and receptive state, and it is through the medium of dreams that your familiar will deliver the message. You will need your cauldron, an object representing your familiar spirit (revisit the previous paragraphs for some ideas), a piece of paper, a pen, and frankincense smoke. It helps to know this person's date of birth or even their place of residence; that way, you can specify who they are. (There can be many people with one name, after all.) Burn the frankincense, and as the smoke rises, allow yourself to get into a trance state. Close your eyes and take a few deep breaths. Allow all of your muscles to relax. Call your familiar by name. If you do not know it yet, simply say:

*Blessed familiar, friend of mine, fly forth
and be here with me in this time.*

Allow it to come to you; you may picture its form flying toward you, over the smoke which is meant to give it strength. When ready, open your eyes. State aloud what it is you wish to convey to this person. For example:

*I want for Jane Doe—born November 1, 1990—
to know that I am thinking of her, it has been
forever since we've talked. She moved away and
doesn't use Facebook or anything. I have no other
way to contact her. Please aid me in this.*

Now, write it all down on the paper, thinking carefully about your message. Like writing an email or a letter, clarity is key. When done, read the message out loud. Fold it away from you to symbolize the message leaving your hands and going into the mind of this person. Put it to a flame and drop it into the cauldron, allowing it to burn. As the smoke rises, take the item representing the familiar spirit in your right hand and hold it over the smoke. Say aloud:

*Blessed familiar, friend of mine, send my message
on this date and time. Spread your wings and fly
through the air, relay my message and get it there!*

End the ritual and be sure to provide offerings to your familiar.

If your familiar takes the form of a land animal, you can use the virtues of Earth, physicality, and materialization to manifest a physical object into your life. This works by telling your familiar what it is you need or want; they will go forth and find it for you in their own mysterious way. You will need patchouli incense, ideal for physical manifestation. In addition to this, acquire a black candle—using the color's virtues of *drawing in*—as well as a symbol of the Earth's black soil. Lastly, you'll need a representation of your familiar. Light the incense and then the black candle. Say aloud:

> *Creature of wax, soil's black; come forth here,*
> *through the earth in a crack. Blessed familiar, come*
> *to my aid; my wish and will is already made.*

Close your eyes and let your mind wander, entering a trance state to facilitate communion with this familiar. Since this is an earthbound familiar, imagine it rising up from the ground to greet you. When you feel its presence, open your eyes and hold onto the object representing it. Speak aloud what it is that you wish to have in your life. For example, you could say how you are in need of a brand-new laptop because the one you have is five years old and starting to break down; or maybe you need a bigger TV so that you can entertain guests better when they visit. Whatever it is, be as clear as possible. As you speak, you are speaking your desire into existence—literally. Let the magic of your voice carry and your familiar pick it up in a feedback loop of sorts. Imagine that the object is right in front of you. When you've exhausted the desire, put the object down and state aloud:

> *Blessed familiar, my will is made; shall it*
> *come true with your generous aid.*

Leave offerings for your familiar and end the spell.

If your familiar can swim or is primarily aquatic, you can harness the powers of water by way of divination. Fill your cauldron with water, then set one black candle and one white candle behind it. The white candle should be on the right, the black on the left. You will also need a representation of your familiar. This is similar to the scrying procedure I gave in the previous chapter, "To See, Hear, Feel, and Know," but this time, you'll be enlisting a familiar's help. Light an incense with aquatic qualities, such as jasmine. (Jasmine is generally amazing for divinatory purposes and helps achieve prophetic dreams, which will come into play later.) Hold the representation of your familiar in your left hand. Get yourself into a trance state, relaxing all of your muscles and breathing steadily and slowly. When ready, light the black and then the white candle, saying:

> *Two flames together, darkness and light; come together*
> *to form visions so bright. Blessed familiar, show me*
> *the way; help me see clearly beyond the gray.*

Then, gaze into the water. You may even see the schema of your familiar in the water; this means that they are present and aiding you. As with regular scrying, let the images form. Take note of anything important your familiar is showing you. Take your time with this process; your familiar may have a lot to say, and that is alright. Sometimes, they may not have too much to say; that is alright too. When finished, still holding the item in your left hand, put your right palm over the cauldron and say:

> *Waters of life, womb and tomb; thanks for all*
> *you've shown in this room. Blessed familiar, away*
> *you swim; but remain close and within.*

End the rite and provide offerings for your familiar.

FINAL THOUGHTS

Don't think that just because you already have three cats that they're your familiars—they're not, sad to say. Again, familiars are *spirits* bestowed upon you by the powers that be.

Always bear in mind that having familiars is not a game. It is important that you maintain some type of control over them so that they serve you well and how they are supposed to. As I mentioned previously, a give-and-take dynamic is important with most kinds of spirit work, but with a familiar, it is different in that they are there to serve you. For example, if you have a pet dog, you need to train it to behave in an agreeable manner, lest they pee on your carpet or rip up your couch pillows. When they behave and do things you want them to do, you give them a treat. Make sure you are clear and concise in what you want your familiars to do for you. If not, they have minds of their own—and will run amok.

THE GREEN WORLD

Humanity has always had a profound relationship with the natural world. Nature has provided us a means of survival—and still does. In particular, our interactions with plants have been both practical and magical. Plants in general reflect the dual nature of the Old Craft itself in that they have the capacity to kill as much as they have it in them to heal. They also have roots that extend into the ground below, with branches, leaves, flowers, or fruits growing out toward the sky. Through careful study of the various plants that exist in this world, a practitioner of the Old Craft can discern what to use and when to use it. Herbalism deserves its own book in and of itself—but let this chapter be a cohesive guide to utilizing them in your own Craft. It is crucial that you exercise caution and prudence when working with herbalism, especially for medicinal use. Be thorough in your research of botanicals and their properties. Always consult with a physician before making any decisions about your health regimen. And of course, nothing in this chapter is a substitute for medical advice you would otherwise receive from a qualified medical practitioner.

Plants have been used the world over for thousands of years, and it is through trial and error that humans have been able to learn what is helpful and what is harmful. Ancient Greece is where we first notice a concrete connection between Witches and the green world—one name used for them was *pharmakeute*, meaning "plant person," which further came from the word *pharmakis*. This is also the root word for *pharmacy*. The *pharmakeute* were well-versed in a secret knowledge of herbs that modern-day doctors could only dream about. They not only healed, but they could kill; their knowledge of plants extended to the most dreadful of poisons. Later in Ancient Rome, we see the similar *venefica*, or "poisoner," a highly misunderstood figure.[51] Yes, she could deal her poisons to interested buyers for a price, but she also needed to know the healing properties of certain plants in order to make antidotes.

To this day, the traditional doctors of China and India take care to know the proper use of herbs in order to help patients. Many well-known pharmaceutical products come from plants, even the deadliest of species. Atropine, which is extracted from the belladonna plant, is used by ophthalmologists today to assist in dilating the eyes during examinations. If injected, it is highly useful in certain operations to dry up saliva and other fluids in the respiratory tract.[52] Digoxin, derived from foxglove, is used in treating arrythmias and heart failure.[53] Aspirin is a common pain reliever that comes from willow bark.[54] Penicillin, the revolutionary antibiotic that became widely available in 1945, is derived from fungi and used to treat a myriad of bacterial infections.[55] Morphine is a powerful, potentially addictive painkiller which is produced by the opium poppy. This plant also has a hand

51 Grimassi, Raven. Grimoire of the Thorn-Blooded Witch: Mastering the Five Arts of Old World Witchery. Weiser Books, 2014.

52 "Atropine Injection." Cleveland Clinic, my.clevelandclinic.org/health/drugs/19824-atropine-injection.

53 David, Marie Nicole V., and Mrin Shetty. "Digoxin." National Library of Medicine, 19 Jan. 2023, ncbi.nlm.nih.gov/books/NBK556025/.

54 Desborough, Michael J. R., and David M. Keeling. "The Aspirin Story - from Willow to Wonder Drug." *British Journal of Haematology*, vol. 177, no. 5, 20 Jan. 2017, pp. 674–683, doi: 10.1111/bjh.14520

55 Newman, Tim. "How Do Penicillins Work?" MedicalNewsToday, 30 July 2018, medicalnewstoday.com/articles/216798#history.

in producing codeine, which is popular for treating coughs.[56] Even in modern medicine, doctors need to know *what* to do and *what not* to do in order to help their patients live as full and healthy lives as possible.

Of course, times and morality have certainly changed, yet it still seems that the doctor is more respected than the local sages simply because they have a degree and years of schooling. Ironically, it takes a practitioner of the Old Craft years to be proficient in dealing with the green world in its many aspects—so what is the actual difference? Aside from a modern doctor's reliance on science and hard empiricism, not very much at all.

My journey with the green world began before I even started down my path in Witchcraft. If astrology was my first love, herbalism became my second. I was so fascinated to learn as an eight-year-old that plants could be used as medicine. When I officially began practice and study at twelve, I studied herbalism the *hardest;* I kept detailed notes on what each plant could be used for. As years went by, herbs and plants became a huge part of my practice, and I learned to interact with their spirits through my spellwork. In some ways, I also began incorporating them into my personal health regimen in order to avoid relying too much on mass-produced, synthetic drugs.[57] I was a loner as a child, not that it was really my fault. That happens sometimes when you find people often reject you from social situations. When going to the park, I would sit under this particular tree; at its roots, I felt safe, comfortable, and grounded. At recess, as young as the second grade, we were told "don't go into the trees," yet I spent many a session sitting there, looking into them and wondering what it would be like if

---

56 "Opium Poppy." Drug Enforcement Administration Museum, museum.dea.gov/exhibits/online-exhibits/cannabis-coca-and-poppy-natures-addictive-plants/opium-poppy#:~:text=Morphine%3A%20In%201803%2C%20morphine%2C.

57 Note: Always consult with a physician before making any such changes to your health regimen. This book and its contents are not a replacement for medical advice.

I broke the rules just *one* time. Even now as an adult, I find extreme comfort and belonging beneath the drooping, graceful arms of the willow that hangs over a footbridge on the way out of a local hiking trail.

When starting with herbalism, you may be tempted to buy a bunch of relatively tame plant species to experiment with, such as lavender or rosemary. This is valid. I, too, still buy herbs when they are not in season around where I am. However, there is *nothing* like going outside and interacting with living, breathing plants. I've already mentioned that most Witches believe that all things have their own spirits, and plants are no exception. They are, after all, alive. Plant spirits are to be treated with respect, and you will know deep down if a plant isn't willing to give up some of their leaves for you or your work. Respect the plant's wishes and move on to a different one. When harvesting your own plants, make sure you know *exactly* what to look for! Do your research beforehand by reading books and studying diagrams. Using a local example, fleabane and daisies look extremely similar and may be associated with protection or chastity, but one is poisonous. If you are making something meant for internal consumption, choosing wisely could mean the difference between no harm done and a trip to the emergency room.

It's important to understand the parts of a plant used in magic. The *root*—which anchors a plant or tree into the soil—is associated with the underworld, the source and final destination of all things. It's used in spells meant to control or bind. The *seed* represents regeneration and creation, while the *leaf*—often called the "hands" of a plant—usually adds potency. The *stem* is the plant's structural symbol of duality and unification; when you look at most plants, the stem is where all branches unite. It is known as the "body" of the plant, where nutrients and water are sucked up through the soil in order to help nourish it. *Branches* on trees and other plants represent the heavens, the world above. *Flowers* are utilized in works of beauty, fruition, and attraction. Lastly, the *fruit* of a plant symbolizes completion and sacrifice. In this structure, we can conceptualize a singular plant as a physical axiom between the heavens and the underworld, rooted into place by all of its life. Another important part of a tree or herb is the *sap*, which is considered its "blood."[58]

VIRTUES OF PLANTS AND TREES

While much more complicated in nature, determining the virtues of plants is an important part of interacting with their individual spirits. When we talk about virtues, we usually do so in terms of planetary influences, though also the values associated with each part of a plant. In understanding the ruling associations of the planets within our solar system, we can apply them to plants.

Botanicals that correspond to the sun usually have bright colors and fresh, cleansing scents, as well as grow high, as if to meet the sun itself. Examples include cinquefoil, heliotrope, and sunflowers. Those that are associated with the moon fare well in the shade; evening primrose, cyclamens, and lilies are all lunar-oriented plants. Lunar botanicals also have the quality of fantasy and dream-like states of consciousness, such as mugwort and datura.

As for plants corresponding with Mercury, they have hollow stems with fragile leaves or buds easily swayed by the wind—lavender, fennel, and thyme are just a few in this category. Venusian plants often bear fruit, such as apples, pears, and peaches, or have fragrant flowers such as roses and gardenias. Those with Martian attributes are potent, have a visible defense mechanism (like thorns), and burn the skin or respiratory tract if burnt. These plants also produce potent ingredients that most of us use to improve recipes—peppers, basil, and onions all belong in this group.

---

58 Schulke, Daniel A. *Viridarium Umbris.* Xoanon Publishing, 2005.

Jovian plants, corresponding with Jupiter, have the tendency to produce nuts or seeds. They also tend to be very large or thick in structure—oak trees are Jovian, as are nutmeg and juniper. Plants ruled by Saturn tend to be baneful and fatally toxic, so use them wisely; such species include belladonna, aconitum, and mandrake. The outer planets also have their botanical associations. For example, those ruled by Uranus tend to be exotic, rare, and brightly colored, reflecting the spirit of eccentricity the planetary influence bears. Pokeweed and bryony are examples of Uranian plants. Neptunian botanicals are of the aquatic variety, such as kelp, algae, and water lilies. Last but not least, those ruled by Pluto are very similar to those ruled by Saturn in that Plutonian plants tend to be poisonous, the primary difference being that Plutonian botanicals have deep roots and other hidden qualities. Species in this category include nightshade and bindweed.

Elemental attributes are also to be considered when selecting species to use in your magical workings and rituals. For more on the elemental correspondences in context of the Circle of Art, go to Chapter Five, "The Circle of Art and Sacred Spaces." Earthen plants may sound like an oxymoron because plants grow in the earth, but certain plants like patchouli have this property because their smell is almost like that of fresh soil. Most food products, like corn, barley and wheat also correspond to this element, as well as moss and lichen species. When considering fiery plants, look to species that have a stinging or otherwise intense quality, like peppers, nettles, and cinnamon. Aquatic plants like kelp, lotuses, and seaweed correspond to the water element for obvious reasons, but so do plants that grow on dry land, like lobelia and periwinkle. Plants that have air-like qualities possess fine veins, fragile leaves, and are very Mercurial—lavender is one such plant, as are dill, peppermint, and yarrow.

Of course, classifying the virtues of the green world's inhabitants is more complicated than what a book like this will tell you. Sometimes, planetary and elemental qualities will mix, and other times a plant may have more than one cosmic ruling.

It happens. Humans in themselves are complex creatures with spirits of their own. So are plants—go out there and interact with them! Let them teach you.

Harvesting for Use

How do we get plant parts to use in magic or medicine? We have to take them from the plants themselves. However, this is not an invitation for you to venture out into the wilderness behind your backyard and snatch up every whole plant you see to make a collection. In fact, doing just that is extremely offensive. It is always a good idea to bring offerings with you when you are gathering plants, herbs, or even so much as the bark off a tree. In the times of the Anglo-Saxons, it was customary to sing to a plant, or speak a charm of praise to that from which you were taking. A prime example of this is the Nine Herbs Charm, where the eponymous nine herbs were sung to in order to harness their healing powers.[59]

If taking physical offerings with you, bring something restorative, even if it is water. Food items are also good to bring and present to a plant. However, avoid wine or anything with salt at all costs—these can poison not only the plant, but the land on which it grows. Your blood may also serve as an offering; in fact, in my personal experience, some plants will automatically take it as such if you touch them. Be sure that if the plant has thorns, its toxicity is not enough to kill you. For example, definitely avoid taking anything from a blackthorn bush with your bare hands—thorns from that tree can inflict dire consequences like blood poisoning and sepsis. Baneful plants should always be given special attention, so wear gloves when handling them and bag them separately. When harvesting from a plant, using a white-handled knife is customary, but

---

59 Cameron, Malcolm Laurence. *Anglo-Saxon Medicine.* Cambridge University Press, 1993.

using your own hands on non-hazardous, fragile plants will do in a pinch. Usually, bits and pieces of a plant are taken such as leaves, fruits, bark shavings, or off-shooting stems—but never the *entire* plant unless there is great need. A rule of thumb to follow is to only harvest from a plant when there is an abundance of said plant in the surrounding area. If it comes to needing the entire plant, you are essentially killing it. Thus, it is important to give substantial offerings or, even better, plant new seeds in its place. A life for a life. However, in doing this, make sure that you are not introducing an invasive species to the area. That will only cause more harm than good.

When approaching a plant, make sure it is exactly what you're seeking—study diagrams, or take the newfangled approach of using apps specially made to identify members of the plant kingdom through a high-quality photo. Identify the location of this plant and examine it. If it is a plant that will not irritate the skin upon touch, you may reach out to caress the plant. Greet it, speak to it, and analyze its unique features. You will know, intuitively, if you can harvest parts from it. If you get an instinctual gut feeling *not* to, avoid that plant and move on. Also, it's not wise to harvest the decayed or dead parts of a plant. The parts must be green and healthy. If the plant spirit lets you take from it, take only what you need, and thank it for its sacrifice. At the roots, pour water as an offering or leave a piece of food in gratitude.

RESINS

Resin is the sap of a tree, synonymous to the blood in a mammal. It holds highly potent properties when used in anything, whether carried on your person or burnt as incense. Much like blood shed from a human or animal holds their very life force, resin does so for the tree from which it comes.

- **Myrrh** is a resin used since ancient times, deriving from the tree genus *Commiphora.* There is evidence it has been used to embalm mummies in ancient Egypt, giving this resin a strong connection to the realm of the dead and the underworld.[60] Myrrh is a feminine resin and can be used in rites of lunar offerings. In history, Isis was the deity that myrrh was most often offered to.[61] It is used for protection, consecration, working with the dead, and to attune oneself to other realms. When burnt along with frankincense, it creates a great altar incense blend for general use.

- **Frankincense** is also a time-honored resin used for incense, a perfect opposite to the aforementioned resin, myrrh. It possesses a masculine vibration associated with the sun and is used for rites involving protection, exorcism, and consecration. It comes from the tree genus *Boswellia* and is synonymous with olibanum. This resin has a long history, having been used on the Arabian Peninsula for over six thousand years; it was introduced to Europe during the Crusades.[62]

- **Copal** is derived from the copal tree (*Protium copal*) and has a long history of use among the Aztecs and Mayans. In the present day, it is used for Day of the Dead celebrations in Mexico. This resin is used for workings having to do with love, amiability, and purification.

- **Dragon's blood** is a popular scent, but the true form of its resin is hard to properly source—let alone come by. It comes from multiple genuses of trees that occur naturally in Southeast Asia, such as Dracaena. Specific trees include *Dracaena cinnabari* and *Dracaena draco*. Other tree species outside of this genus also produce dragon's

60 Schulke, Daniel A. *Viridarium Umbris.* Xoanon Publishing, 2005.

61 Isidora. "Isis & the Magic of Myrrh." Isiopolis, 20 July 2013, isiopolis. com/2013/07/20/isis-the-magic-of-myrrh/.

62 "Cross-Cultural Trade and Cultural Exchange during the Crusades." The Sultan and the Saint, 2019, sultanandthesaintfilm.com/education/ cross-cultural-trade-cultural-exchange-crusades/.

blood, such as *Calamus draco* and *Pterocarpus officianalis*. Dragon's blood is powerful; thus, when added to your spellwork, it adds its potency to the mix. It is also great for protection and banishing work.

- **Pine** resin, on the other hand, is a bit easier to come by if you live in the woodlands, where coniferous trees are abundant. It is a very sweet but strong-smelling resin that is perfect for healing and deep cleansing; burning even the needles in a room where someone is sick can help clear the air of impurities. Pine resin can also be used to send back spells, increase fertility, preserve longevity, and invoke financial prosperity.

- **Amber** is a fossilized resin from ancient trees. According to Pliny the Elder, amber comes from fossilized pine trees.[63] However, since it can be found in tropical regions like the Dominican Republic, and pine trees do not grow there, amber could come from a variety of trees. In the world today, the Baltic regions and Eastern Europe are famous for their abundance of amber; blue amber naturally occurs in the Dominican Republic. Amber can be worn as jewelry, and it's very powerful all-around in matters of health, vitality, and beauty. It also serves to connect us to the primal and ancient. In Norse mythology, the goddess Freyja is associated with this resin because it was believed that after her lover was killed, her tears were of amber—though some versions of the story say that her tears were gold instead. Amber incense as we know it today is in fact a mixture, because burning a fossilized resin is not going to smell great after millions of years. Amber is best used in matters of love, health, protection, psychic enhancement, and good fortune.

- **Storax** (or styrax) is a resin that comes from the tree *Liquidambar orientalis*, or the oriental sweetgum tree. It is

63 Thayer, Bill. "Pliny the Elder: the Natural History." penelope.uchicago.edu/thayer/e/roman/texts/pliny_the_elder/home.html.

an ideal resin to use when embarking on spirit work, astral travel, or prosperity.

- **Galbanum**—coming from the genus Ferula—is aromatic but has a bitter, disagreeable taste. It has a long history of use in the Middle East, especially since it was used as an incense offering in ancient Hebrew temples. Outside of organized religion, galbanum is used for work involving spirits or psychic enhancement.
- **Opoponax** also has a long history of use and is the only resin on this list deriving from a genus of the same name. It has been used in perfumery for ages and works best in magic involving necromancy, or in helping a practitioner meditate and retain knowledge.

BANEFUL PLANTS

While medicine and benefice can be found in the many different plant species on this earth, there are also plants that are extremely harmful to ingest or even touch. Do *not* attempt to use these plants unless you are experienced and have researched them well. The list below is here as a reference, because as a practitioner of the Old Craft, you have two hands. One is to bless and heal; the other is to curse and harm. Be mindful that these plants are not specific to one region in the world. These plant spirits have a lot to teach, but you must approach them with caution, prudence, and knowledge. Consider yourself warned:

- **Crocus** is a hardy plant first spotted through the winter snows as spring begins; its lovely purple color is eye-catching, and it can be used for love and friendship, as well as for settling disputes and maintaining peace.
- **Morning glory** can be used for aid in astral travel, divination, and dreamwork for those who have mastered her secrets—and, perhaps, gotten used to her poison.

- **Oleander,** a popular bush in the American South, has long been used as a potent poison. Fittingly, it has a long history of lore, from the legend of St. Joseph using the plant to pick bridegrooms for the Virgin Mary to symbolizing the harmony of the universe according to Pythagoras. Oleander can be used for beauty, courage, remembering the dead, and separation.
- **Buttercup** can be employed in prosperity or career work.
- **Hyacinth** can help with matters of love and repelling nightmares.
- **Wisteria tree** is helpful in emotional healing, inspiration, beauty, and grace.
- **Larkspurs** are great for magic involving the protection of animals and for keeping specters at bay.
- **Philodendron** is a common house plant, and while it is easy to care for, it is not meant for consumption; however, you may see fit to use this plant for forgiveness and abundance-related spells.
- **Daffodils,** one of the most popular springtime flowers, can be used for prosperity and matters involving love. Wearing them near your heart can draw love, but do your part to make sure it's not unreciprocated.
- **Tobacco**—commonly a source of addiction for those unaware of its true nature—is a carcinogen only exacerbated by the thousands of chemicals found in products like cigarettes. This plant can be given as an offering and used in curses or money spells. In rituals where it is respectfully smoked, it is a chance for a Witch to get "closer to death," so to speak, communing with departed spirits while also cherishing life in that space between spaces.

Sometimes, baneful plants bear fruit such as berries. The list that follows contains some examples, as New England has a fair share of toxic plants that grow berries:

- **Rosary peas** resemble ladybugs—especially the seeds—and can be used to craft amulets.
- **Mistletoe** has a long history in the mythologies of Europe. It was greatly revered by the Celtic people, and according to lore from the British Isles, it should never touch the ground[64] when being harvested. In Norse mythology, Loki killed Balder by proxy through means of manipulating the blind god Hod to shoot him with it. It can be used to protect from lightning and to promote male fertility.
- **Holly** is another potent plant that protects from all kinds of harmful influences, including storms.
- **Yew** berries look almost plastic, and the entire tree is deadly. Despite its associations with necromancy, the tree can also be used in works of longevity, perseverance, and immortality. The yew tree may lose a branch, but then it will only grow back as part of the tree, thus continuing a cycle.
- **Chinaberry** seeds and berries can be carried for good luck.
- **Doll's eyes,** also known as "white baneberry," have a distinctive red stem upon which white berries with black spots grow. They can be used in banishing magic or in rituals honoring the dead. Taking into account their appearance, they can also be used for clarity of vision and sight, providing an ability to see the truth in all matters.

This section would not be complete without mentioning the cornerstones of baneful plants within the Old Craft. These plants have a very long history in European Witchcraft for being used in flying ointments, which aid in spirit flight. They are applied to pulse points and otherwise sensitive parts of the body so that the chemical effects can easily enter the bloodstream. Again, a word of caution to those not used to the effects of these fatal poisons. An interesting fact about these

---

64 Schulke, Daniel A. *Viridarium Umbris.* Xoanon Publishing, 2005.

plants is that most belong to the family *Solanacae*, along with potatoes, eggplant, and tomatoes.

- **Belladonna** is the most famous of all witching herbs. It has pitch-black berries and mauve-colored flowers that serve as its trademark. It is employed in works of war, cursing, honoring the dead, and ironically, healing. Some medicinal uses of this plant by expert herbalists include easing muscle spasms and relieving aches; for ophthalmologists, it is used (in the form of atropine sulfate) to dilate the pupils for better examination.
- **Foxglove,** otherwise known as "digitalis," is by far and large a plant associated with the Fae Folk. Thus, it is appropriate for use in working with them. The plant also may be used to commune with the spirit realm. Foxglove, medicinally, has been used to treat certain heart conditions—as mentioned previously, digoxin is largely derived from this botanical.
- **Mandrake** roots are also famous for use among Witches, often for love spells, rendering invisibility, and dreaming true if put under a pillow. The mandrake root resembles a human form with arms and legs; thus, it is an ideal component for sympathetic magic. According to folklore, harvesting a mandrake can be dangerous due to the frequency of its screams when pulled from the ground, in addition to the fact that it is poisonous. Thus, an old dog was usually tasked with digging it up only to die shortly after. This was done by tying one end of a rope around the dog and the other end to the top of the mandrake; the dog would be made to run, pulling it out of the ground as a result.[65] Mandrake is also a very popular plant familiar due to its anthropomorphic shape.

---

65 Conway, David. *Magic: An Occult Primer: 50 Year Anniversary Edition.* The Witches' Almanac, 2022.

- **Hemlock** is written about in the next section as a well-known local New England plant, but it also makes the list of baneful herbs because of its use in flying ointments. Other uses include empowering ritual blades, destroying one's sex drive, and rituals of restriction or hexing.
- **Hellebore** is distinctive with its leathery petals and colors ranging from purple-red to black, yellow, and even white. In magic, it is employed for necromancy and banishing magic. The Greeks believed it to be a cure for insanity, associating it with mental and emotional health.
- **Datura** has large flowers that can grow to the size of your hand. This plant can be used for all kinds of spirit work or travel, as well as for love magic, shapeshifting, hexes, and curses. Being a powerful hallucinogen, datura has made headlines in modern news because people wanting to experiment with recreational drugs were foolish enough to ingest it,[66] only to have drug-induced psychosis or succumb to the plant's unforgiving spirit. It has also been used by organized crime groups—particularly in South America—who deal in drugs like scopolamine.[67] Thus, I strongly advise against using this plant at all if you have a history of psychosis or other severe mental health problems.
- **Aconite** is another plant heavily associated with the Fae Folk. Its folk name *wolfsbane* comes from its use as protection from wolves at one point. Perhaps this is because the amount of poison needed to kill a predatory wolf in the wild is so small, that shepherds planted them in their land far enough to keep their flocks safe but within range for a wolf to eat the plant and die. In magic, aconite can be used to

---

66 Cooke, Justin. "Datura: Risks, Experience & Trip Reports." *Tripsitter*, 20 Mar. 2021, tripsitter.com/datura/.

67 Harker, Joe. "'World's Scariest Drug' Has Been Used by Organised Crime Gangs." UNILAD, 22 Aug. 2022, unilad.com/news/worlds-scariest-drug-crime-gangs-20220822.

help one become invisible or for protection, hexes, and curses. Since this plant is such a potent poison, I'd advise against using it unless you are experienced or under the supervision of an expert herbalist.

Useful Magical Plants

The following list includes plants that not only grow in New England, but in other regions with similar climates. This list is by no means complete, as it is based on my own local foraging trips. There are thousands of species and variations across my region of the US, but here are a few good ones to know:

- **Lavender** is usually an adornment perennial found in gardens and warm temperatures. Summers in New England can be quite hot, so growing these in your garden is a snap. In magic, they are famously used for love spells, especially in attracting a potential partner (most notably a man to a woman in historical texts). Lavender is also great to use for peaceful sleep and for calming anxiety; it also makes an excellent tea. In the Renaissance, this herb was paired with rosemary and thought to preserve chastity.
- **Honeysuckles** are another garden favorite, but don't let the name fool you. If you ingest honeysuckle, you may feel very sick or experience a rapid heartbeat. If you touch certain varieties, you may get a slight rash on your skin. This plant is great for money magic, ensuring financial gain and maintenance. If it grows outside your home, it is considered very good luck. Honeysuckle is also an ideal plant for newlyweds to have around, helping them along to a great life together.
- **Bindweed** is exactly as it sounds. I observe this plant growing over bushes in vine-like formations. Related to the toxic morning glory, it is invasive and parasitic, so *do not* voluntarily grow this in your garden. Due to the

nature of this plant, it is good to use in curses and hexes. If you try to uproot a bindweed, the deeper roots could remain, causing it to grow back—this is a fact that ties it with works of regeneration and perseverance. As the name also suggests, it is a good plant spirit to employ for binding as well as for making bridges between worlds.

- **Pokeweed,** or simply *poke*, is a very eye-catching plant. When mature, it is like a large, purply bush. Up close, you'll see magenta-colored stems and the black berries that grow on them. This member of the green world is highly toxic, and the berries are bitter and smell terrible. Unripe berries can be cooked and made into a type of jelly for consumption. Otherwise, mature berries make a lovely ink for spellwork. Pokeweed works wonders in banishing and exorcism, as well as protection.
- **Aster** is a perennial that looks like a daisy, except it has light purple petals. Last year, at the time of writing this book, we had an abundance of these flowers growing wild in my area. You can utilize this plant in love spells in addition to exacting gentle justice and granting wishes.
- **Stinging nettle** is a common plant species in most temperate environments, and I've often come across it while hiking in the woods. It is easy to spot with its distinctive leaves; up close, you can see the tiny hairs that—were you to touch them—would sting you. This species is great for protection and countermagic, as well as healing and inciting lust. Nettles, despite the stinging hairs on their leaves, can be boiled and made into a tea.
- **Crabapples** remind me of school projects in kindergarten around the time the year started. They are not edible when raw, but when cooked, they can be made into jelly and cider. The latter of these makes a great offering to the Fae Folk around autumn. Crabapples are also good to use for love spells.
- **Loosestrife** smells sweet and almost candy-like, and while they come in a variety of colors, I have personally seen

them in shades of blue and purple. These are great for the bees; for Witches, they're useful in works involving peace, protection, amiability, and love. Loosestrife can also be employed in the home to ward away evil spirits and to keep all within happy and content.

- **Hemlock** is a lookalike to the next plant on this list, and it is important to note how poisonous this plant is. Hemlock is traditionally associated with unguents that help the user fly or astral project; if the fresh flowers are rubbed on a ritual blade, they help empower it before use. Hemlock is also known for decreasing one's sex drive, either as part of a baneful working against someone or to maintain chastity in yourself.

- **Queen Anne's Lace,** or *wild carrot,* greatly resembles hemlock. The main difference I have noticed is how the buds grow. On Queen Anne's lace, the buds grow tighter together, whereas hemlock's buds are spaced further apart. This plant is associated with purity and light—and is thus employed for beauty and fertility. A flower crown can be made from this plant and placed on the head of a pregnant woman to ensure a safe delivery and a healthy baby.

- **Goldenrod** is a plant that is hard to miss; its yellow flowers grow in stalk-like clusters, and I usually see them peeking over fences on lawns or freely among trails. Legend has it that goldenrods point in the direction of wealth and treasures. When this plant unexpectedly grows on someone's property, it portends good fortune and luck for the family living there. This amicable plant spirit is ideal for use in magic involving business success, career, money, and good fortune.

- **Annual nightshade,** like bindweed, is invasive and tends to grow within bushes. It is a plant that is hidden in plain sight—if you can spot distinctive purple flower buds and bright red berries, then you know you've found it. It is a resilient plant spirit, surviving even into cold autumn months. I have childhood memories of my father making me spit out annual nightshade as I played outside, not knowing any better about this plant. From that experience, I know that these berries are bitter and nasty, but they do make a great ink. This plant is different than most nightshades; while it is still quite poisonous, it is not quite to the level as belladonna. In magic, this plant is employed for baneful workings as well as protection.

- **Dittander,** a lookalike to yarrow, is a type of dittany that is mostly edible and has white flowers that grow in tight clusters. It is known to grow back even stronger when it is plucked or cut out of a garden; this quality gives it the power of endurance and perseverance. Use this to stand your ground, however you may have to. Being related to dittany, dittander shares uses in magic involving protection or healing.

- **Mugwort,** while not native to New England, does grow around my area and seems like a common weed. I remember going out once to forage for it, only to find that it had been ripped up from the ground by the town. Mugwort is famous for use in magic involving divination, spirit travel, and psychic abilities. It's also a great plant for women to use medicinally to regulate their menstrual cycles.

- **Daisies** evoke images of children on the playground plucking their petals, asking if someone likes them or not; on the last petal, the answer would be said aloud. This flower doesn't just grow in New England, but all over the US. It is used for divination work, as well as for the protection of babies and children. Daisies are also included in certain salad recipes and can serve as garnish for soups.

- **Fleabane** looks a lot like the aforementioned daisy (and also chamomile), but in contrast, it's poisonous and its petals are more so filaments. Fleabane is a natural bug repellant, keeping mites and fleas away. In magic, this plant is to be used for protection. It can also preserve chastity if you sprinkle the petals in your bedsheets. When it comes to spirits, it helps dispel parasitic forces that may cause you bodily harm.

- **Evening primrose** is a glorious yellow wildflower. It can be employed for enchantment and shapeshifting; widely associated with the Fae Folk, it can also be used in communing with the other world— even the dead. The dew from this flower is used in beauty work.

- **Vetch** is known by a variety of names (like *cow vetch* or *bird vetch*). Its flowering nature is surely enchanting. In fact, it can be employed for this type of work, as well as for capturing attention or having influence over someone or something. It comes in colors like purple, blue, or pink. It also serves as a snare for spirits, making it a great ward against such beings if you do not want them around. The scent serves as an aphrodisiac.

- **Blazingstar** is a unique plant I came across one summer, only to learn later that it is native to the eastern US, including New England. It has filaments rather than petals, and its stalk is quite tall for a flower. Its rich purple-blue color reminds me of angelic fire—as if it fell to Earth and became this beautiful plant. It is great when employed in protection work, divination, and psychic enhancement, helping you to open yourself up to higher realms, as well as in improving charisma and eloquence.

- **Dandelions** are considered to be a bothersome weed to most, but like almost every member of the green world, they carry a very strong spirit. They are used for wishes, opening the psychic senses, and for calling forth amicable spirits to aid in constructive works. Dandelions are also great for stimulating creativity and happiness.

- **Dock** is a hardy flowering plant. I have observed it growing in sparse areas near marshy environments. The seeds of this plant are excellent for invoking business success as well as for attracting money, either from said business or other sources. The flowers of this plant—ranging from yellow to a light shade of red—can help with fertility and conception.

- **Lilac** tends to grow around late April into May, and its scent is unmistakable. It is a bush commonly found in gardens. Lilacs can be used for glamouring, attraction, and remembering previous lives. Lilac can also be used offensively and defensively as a potent addition to protection, exorcism, and banishing work.

- **Chicory** is a plant whose root is its most potent part. It has been used as both a medicine and a magical property for quite a long time. In the woods, I will see these just barely grazing the edge of a path, peacefully watching anyone who might pass by. According to lore, this plant is best gathered in complete silence on Midsummer's Eve either at the peak of day or at midnight. Chicory was also thought to make one invisible, to open locks, and to aid in obtaining favors from people in high places. Medicinally, it has been used to treat a variety of gastrointestinal problems.

- **Red clover** is a common plant found anywhere from backyards to forested areas. This plant has historically been used as medicine to alleviate menopausal symptoms and arthritis. An attractor of hard-working bees, red clover also helps attract money as well as beneficial financial situations. Red clover is also good to use in banishing work or inciting lust.

The Green World is a vast expanse filled with diverse life and great power. It is an axiom that includes the heavens above and the great below—and in between, us. We stand on the grass, the stones, and the soil. Just as the very nature of Witches is betwixt and between, humanity itself is as a whole; we are born, we live our lives on the earth, and when we die, we are buried to become part of it again. Thus, it is only natural that the Green World has such an important place in the practice of Witchcraft.

CHAPTER TEN

ONEIRIC VENTURES

Many people, regardless of whether they practice magic, often push dreams to the wayside in favor of the rational mind, physical reality, and the dismissal of imagination. Of course, we cannot ignore why dreams happen in the first place. So much research has been done over the years, and even still, to this day, they mystify scientists. Yet, the general consensus is that dreaming is our brain's way of processing things we perceive in daily life. Dreams occur during the REM—or rapid eye movement—stage of sleep, when our brains are the most active. Experts say that we dream between four and six times a night.[68] Even if we do not remember our dreams, they still occurred. Dreams can last anywhere from four to thirty minutes on average, but despite the placement of these earthly time estimates on dreams, they tend to feel like eternities, don't they? Well, that is also a mystery.

In many ancient civilizations, dreams were an important source of divine inspiration in addition to reflecting our deepest passions, desires, thoughts, feelings, and wishes. Dreams have also been an avenue for the spirit world to communicate with the living, whether it is loved ones who have crossed over or the gods themselves. As mentioned in Chapter Seven, "To See, Hear, Feel, and Know," dreams have been used to interpret the

---

68 "How Long Do Dreams Last?" Healthline, 10 Feb. 2020, healthline.com/health/ how-long-do-dreams-last#how-long-dreams-last.

future, make sense of the past, or shed light on what can be done in the present to alter events of the future. I remember first having prophetic dreams when I was a preteen. I was clued in to what they were because I'd discovered earlier that my mom kept a dream book filled with interpretations. Naturally, she would refer to it if she was confused about any symbols that appeared in her dreams, although she was sharp enough to connect the dots on her own most of the time. In her dreams, she was always visited by our deceased loved ones; alternatively, she would vivid dream around the time someone was going to pass from this world to the next. This is a gift that I inherited from my maternal line.

If you have dreams in a state between wakefulness and sleep, where you can consciously control what takes place or reenter dreams after being awake for a period of time, this is called *lucid dreaming*. Sometimes, dreams that seem like dreams are not actually dreams at all. If you are moving around as though you are awake, able to touch things in the physical, or looking back at your body sleeping in your bed, you're experiencing *astral travel*.

In a dream state, a Witch may not only receive visions of the future or visitations from the spirit world, but also deliver magic into the ether, pay homage to spiritual forces, and receive healing. Being asleep is a very receptive and therefore vulnerable state; in dreams, you can determine if malevolent magic has been placed on you, but you are also the most exposed as a target of others' magic. Signs you've been targeted by a spell vary depending on what was done. When dreamt of, dead animals or parasitic insects like ticks are terrible omens, indicating that a curse may have been put on you. A dream about being a puppet could indicate that you are being influenced by a third party in order to affect a situation so that it goes in their favor. Dreaming of the face of someone you barely know on a constant basis could mean that a love spell was put on you. These are just a few examples, but they're not an invitation to read into every single dream you have. Interpreting dreams is an art; there are many things that go into doing so. It is important not to take things too far out of context—or you will just have a headache. In my own experience, not all dreams have some deeper, esoteric meaning. As mentioned in the beginning of this chapter, dreams are a way for our brains to subconsciously process what we perceive while we are awake and conscious; in those cases, that is all it is.

Oneiric Flight and Lucid Dreaming

The idea that Witches could fly comes from the concept of *spirit flight*—that is, the ability to project one's soul from one's body to perform feats of magic. Witches were said to fly off to the enigmatic Witches' Sabbath, meeting the Devil and the Queen of the Fae. According to inquisitors, this was done either naturally or with aids such as ointments, which we now know were likely made of powerful but fatally poisonous plants like belladonna, monkshood, and foxglove.[69] This ointment would then be applied to an area of the body where things are more readily absorbed into the bloodstream, such as the nether regions—and sometimes even with the help of a broom handle, for purposes of self-gratification in getting to the state of mind needed to leave the physical world. The ointment could have also been applied (at the pulse points) to induce spirit flight while sleeping, perhaps a much safer alternative than the former. However, it is not unheard of for spirit flight to happen naturally. Sometimes, it is not up to you *when* you are out-of-body, as it may happen at any interval during the night.

In fact, you may not fly to meet a bunch of other Witches in an astral gathering. You may go someplace else entirely, as the

---

69 della Porta, Giambattista. *Natural Magick by John Baptista Porta, a Neapolitane.* Legare Street Press, 2021.

world of spirit is truly limitless and timeless. You can visit any place in the physical realm or other worlds—and experience the past, present, and future. Some realms truly are unearthly, with creatures and settings that do not exist in our known world. For instance, I remember being in spirit flight during a dream once: it was night, with hues of purple and blue, and I hovered over gargantuan daturas and moonflowers. There are other times you may find yourself wandering around your apartment at three in the morning, without even having to leave your bed. This may sound impossible, but as I mentioned, most people have out-of-body experiences at least once in their lifetime. In fact, you can *train* your mind and consciousness to leave your body. Here is a simple start for those brand-new to the practice.

You need to be in a state of consciousness that is in between sleep and wakefulness. A good time to practice this is very early in the morning if you happen to wake up, or at night as you are trying to fall asleep. Once your eyes have been open for a bit, let your fatigue take over. Close your eyes, but keep your mind awake enough to project your consciousness out of your body. Relax every muscle; even if you feel an itch, resist the urge to scratch it.

With your eyes closed and all muscles relaxed and still, imagine your body is like an ice cube tray, a mold of your astral form. Starting with your legs, imagine them loosening enough to "pop out" of this metaphorical ice cube tray. Then, your hands and arms in the same fashion; in your mind's eye, see your surroundings but also your limbs out of your physical body. Your head and neck come next; project your consciousness so that the top of your body starts to float. Let your torso follow. You may feel like you are floating—this is a sign you are out-of-body. You can move around however you wish from this point, though a good starting point is your immediate surroundings. If your physical body is on your bed, then float around to other areas in your room—your dresser, your desk, your doorway. Take in your surroundings. You may even turn to see your physical body asleep.

As you progress and improve, you can send your astral body anywhere—to your workplace, to a favorite public place such as a café you frequent or your favorite store, to visit someone (though they may not even know you're there). Astral projection could start happening beyond your control, and that is okay. Usually, once you are in this stream of consciousness, you are able to control where you go anyhow. This brings us to our next topic of lucid dreaming.

Lucid dreaming does not always go hand in hand with spirit flight, but it is a type of extremely vivid dreaming where you control the events in the dream. As mentioned previously, you're actually able to reenter dreams if you wake up for a short time, picking up where you left off. It obviously won't work if you had the dream three nights before and want to reenter it; it's just not possible. This is because the window between being asleep and being fully awake is a small one. As you wake up, your mind fills with other things, and the dream you had gets pushed into your subconscious. You are much more receptive when in a hypnogogic state, so it is important to take advantage of this brief window of time between sleeping and wakefulness.

You can also have lucid dreaming happen spontaneously, where your brain recognizes that you are partially conscious even in the deepest stages of sleep. If this happens, see what you can do to alter the course of your dream. Walk around, pick something up, look around, and take in the visuals. Whenever I have personally experienced this, it happens when I am just about to wake up, but I realize that I am still in a dream and can do things within that state of mind; then, I am fully asleep again. I compare the sensation to being completely underwater, almost coming up for air, and then going back down under the surface.

If you find yourself jolted awake and want to reenter a dream, try to get into the same state of mind you'd be in when trying to astral project—a state between being awake and asleep. This is best achieved in the very early morning, if you find yourself awakening at that time for whatever reason.

Once your eyes feel heavy enough, go with it. Let them close while you pinpoint a part of your previous dream that you wish to reenter. Make sure that you can *vividly* remember it: Who was there? Where were you? Was there one object you fixed on in your environment? Use these questions to bring you back into that space as you fall asleep. This will not work as well if you cannot remember your dream.

Protection during Sleep

As mentioned, it is during sleep that you are the most vulnerable to others' magic. This is not intended to trigger paranoia, but it is always good to be prepared. Here are some helpful things to try out in order to protect you as you sleep.

Assemble a cross from the twigs or branches of a willow tree—willows have a connection to water, the spirit world, the subconscious, and dreams, making them ideal for protection during sleep. Fasten the center of the cross with a white ribbon, making sure the arms are even in length. Fumigate the cross with opium or poppy seed incense, projecting your will into it all the while. (To clarify, I do not mean *actual* opium; I'm referring to the stick incense variety.) As the smoke rises to greet what you crafted, say:

> *Earthly spirit of the willow, arboreal lady*
> *of the waterside, I ask that you protect me as*
> *I sleep each and every night. So mote it be.*

For added power, kiss the center where you fastened the ribbon, then hang up the cross.

If you have an amulet for general protection that you never take off, wearing it to bed will do just fine to protect you. However, a traditional English way to protect yourself—during sleep and oneiric ventures alike—is by hanging hawthorn berries near the window closest to your bed.[70] This also prevents malevolent practitioners from entering your window via astral travel.

When it comes to interpreting dreams, a dream dictionary is an ideal tool to have at your disposal; you're able to keep a record of your dreams and refer back to it as needed. Journals can be found most anywhere, and there are many dream dictionaries available that are written through cultural, religious, and even philosophical lenses. Select one, and if something sticks out to you once you wake up, take it out and write it down. Relate your dream to what is currently going on in your life. This is a divinatory art called *oneiromancy*, in which dreams are a source of visions, guidance, and where the symbols can be interpreted and applied to your waking life. It is much like a puzzle; you have to put the pieces together in order to create a bigger picture that explains life events and what is to come.

---

70 Sedgwick, Icy. "Hawthorn Folklore: Fairies and the May Day Tree." Icy Sedgwick, 28 Nov. 2020, icysedgwick.com/hawthorn-folklore/.

CHAPTER ELEVEN

PRACTICAL SPELLCRAFT

Spells can be as simple or elaborate as you would like them to be, from crafting implements to just getting a job done. Open yourself to learning practical spellcraft with two of the greatest tools in your arsenal, which also happen to be attached to your body: your hands. They are not only a body part you use on a daily basis to complete tasks, but an extension of your consciousness and will to make magic happen. A spell is defined as a procedure that carries out your will by way of magic. They can vary in the time it takes to do one, the amount of tools or implements needed, and timing by day or hour; all of these things greatly affect a spell's outcome. They are commonly thought to just be words, and while this is true in some cases, most spells within Witchcraft involve more than that.

Spells are a means to an end, and like all ends, there are many means with which to achieve them. They can accomplish a variety of things, and all in their own time. Some manifest quickly; others take longer like the growing of a tree. They can be used to help or to heal, and also to harm or destroy. Many people see magic as a dichotomy of *black* and *white*, but the reality is far more complex than that. I've seen magic that is often considered *black* used to help someone (and have done so myself at times). For example, such spells can aid someone who is stuck in an abusive relationship with an insufferable partner or can exact justice when the authorities will not intervene like they were supposed to. The possibilities are endless and go beyond this concrete way of thinking. To work spells successfully means being able to plan and execute your will to its fullest extent. It also entails strategy and skill, which can only be learned over time.

What sorts of things can you craft and make into magical objects? What can they be used for? Here are several methods of making magic that we will cover in this chapter:

- Spell mixes
- Incense
- Oils
- Inks
- Poppets
- Spell bags

SPELL MIXTURES

Very easy things to create, these are botanical blends made up of leaves, flowers, stems, or roots of plants—mixed for a specific purpose. Sometimes, mixtures can contain powders from other things, such as eggshells or bone meal. They can be used to dress candles, put into spell bags, used as offerings, used to infuse baths, or burnt over charcoal as a loose incense. To create a mixture, you'll need a mortar and pestle, as well as herbs of your choice that relate to your goal.

It is important to remember that whatever herbs you use in your mixture, they should both correspond to what you are trying to achieve and go well together. For example, putting roses and tobacco leaves together for a love spell is not a very good idea; in that same respect, you would not use most baneful herbs for healing spells. By working with plants, you are working with living things—thus, you are also working with their spirits. While adding the herbs into the mortar, say aloud what you want for them to do. That way, you're interacting with the spirits of the plants you're working with and calling upon their virtues in order to help you attain your goal. Providing offerings on your workspace is always good after such interactions.

For spells of gain or attraction, grind your herbs in a clockwise motion in the pestle and mortar. For spells of banishment or destruction, grind them in a counterclockwise motion. If your mortar is large enough to fit your hands, hand mixing them after grinding is a good way to add your intention into it even further. Make sure you are fully focused on the final goal of your working as you do so. When ready, bottle the mixture for future use in a dark-colored jar, or use it right away in a ritual. The reason why I recommend a dark-colored jar, such as brown or amber, is because it preserves the contents for longer and keeps them fresh. Also, light can corrupt and ruin the ingredients stored within. It is even more ideal if you store dark-colored bottles in a dark place.

As you will read below, you can use spell mixtures in most any practical spellcrafting that you do:

- **Love:** For any spell relating to love, mix rose petals (ideal if you use one bud and remove the petals), patchouli leaves, six buds of baby's breath, six forget-me-not flowers, and some myrtle. Prepare this mixture on a Friday during the waxing or full moon.
- **Lust:** To ignite passion and lust, mix patchouli leaves, one vanilla bean, six cherry blossoms, and damiana. This mixture is best prepared on a Tuesday or Friday under the planetary auspices of Mars and Venus. The moon should be waxing or full for best results.
- **Success:** To invoke success in all that you do, mix one bay leaf, cinquefoil, three red clover buds, and one oak leaf. Prepare on a Sunday when the moon is new, waxing, or full.
- **Money:** When working with money matters, mix one bay leaf, bergamot, nutmeg, cinnamon, powdered sage, and gold flecks. Concoct on a Thursday under the

auspices of Jupiter—or on a Sunday, when the moon is waxing or full.

- **Baneful:** When working a hex or curse, use the following mixture. Take a pinch each of poppy seeds, patchouli, wormwood, boneset, tormentil, and chili powder. You can adapt this to suit whatever you wish to happen to your target, but this is the general recipe. It is best prepared on a Saturday evening when the moon is waning or dark.
- **Protection:** When working protections and wards, mix horehound, cayenne pepper powder, chili powder, and ground mistletoe. This mixture can be prepared anytime you need it, but it is particularly potent when prepared on a Tuesday or Saturday beneath the waning or dark moon, during a Saturnian or Martian hour.
- **Wishes:** To achieve your wishes, mix three bay leaves, ground dandelion, and some yarrow. Fix this mixture under the new moon on a Sunday, Monday, or Thursday.
- **Fertility:** Use this mixture in spells meant to help one conceive, be it you or someone else. Gather some dried banana peel, ground mistletoe, a pinch of rice, fennel, and motherwort. This is best prepared during the full moon on a Monday.

INCENSE

Incense has a long history of use in religious rituals, setting the atmosphere or serving as an offering to spirits and deities. While you may find cone or stick incenses to be convenient options, there is nothing quite like making your own. Incenses are not limited to plant matter like roots, bark, or leaves; they have other components like oils and resins. The latter of these makes a great binding agent for looser plant matter. While tutorials exist for creating your own sticks and cones, creating a blend that burns over charcoal discs in a censer is a classic way to craft incense and infuse power into your rituals. In the same way you craft an herbal mixture, tell each component what you want it to do for you. Remember, you are working with the innate spirits of these plants. For gain or increase, grind clockwise. For destruction or reduction, grind counterclockwise. Oils can lend their scent to your incense and act as a binding agent; just note that if you use oils with an herbal mixture, it will bind together in clumps. Make sure it isn't *too* clumpy. A little oil goes a long way.

Take special care with using baneful plants or resins in an incense recipe—if anything, it is best to avoid them as some can cause a lot of physiological damage simply from inhalation. That said, if you choose to employ resins anyway, do so as you would when selecting plants and their parts: according to what you want to achieve with your work. Do you want your incense to heal or purify a space? Resin from a coniferous tree, like pine, would be a good choice. Want to work with the spirits of those who have passed? Opoponax, gum mastic, or galbanum would suffice. Do you desire love or amiability in your life? Choose something like copal or amber. Perhaps you would like an all-purpose resin that will empower any incense that includes it. Although its true form is quite rare and expensive, dragon's blood is an option. Want to honor spirits and entities? For most cases, resins like frankincense, sandalwood, and myrrh work—just make sure you research what scents are appropriate for whom you are honoring. Do you need a financial boon? Storax has properties associated with prosperity. All in all, make sure the virtues of the resin you choose are compatible with the plants that are in the recipe. Resins may be harder to grind, but make sure they are well-mixed with the rest of the plant matter you are using. Then store the incense in a labelled, airtight container; burn it to release its effects.

Below, you'll find a few incense recipes:

- **Divination:** Procure some myrrh resin, damiana, acacia, dittany of Crete, wormwood, mugwort, and eyebright. Use this when scrying or when performing divination.
- **Love:** This recipe calls for dried rose buds that have maintained their fragrance, damiana, a vanilla bean, copal resin, and a few drops of either amber or apricot oil. Use this incense in all love-related matters.
- **Money:** Use this incense when dealing with finances and business. You'll need cinnamon, nutmeg, cedar wood chips, three whole cloves, and allspice.
- **Baneful:** This incense is to be used in hexes or curses. Make sure you burn it in a well-ventilated area, as it is rather noxious and could irritate the respiratory tract. For this recipe, you will need wormwood, asafoetida, cumin, a pinch of cayenne pepper, and myrrh resin.
- **Protection:** This incense is versatile in its use, as there are many things in our lives we can protect. You may use it to protect yourself and those close to you. You may also burn it when enchanting objects meant for protection, as well as around your home and vehicle. Combine mugwort, horehound, agrimony, and vervain with some dragon's blood resin.
- **Cleansing:** Burn this incense when you need to fumigate your home of unwanted or stagnant energy. You may also burn it to cleanse yourself or someone else. Another of its uses is as a pre-cursor to any protection work. Craft it with some angelica root fragments, pine needles, pine resin, cedar wood chips, sifted hyssop, dragon's blood resin, and sandalwood.
- **Healing:** This is a general healing incense—you may tailor the ingredients depending on the condition of the person you are trying to heal. Use pine needles, pine resin, mesquite, life-everlasting, spearmint, and yerba santa.

INKS

Magical inks can be used in the inscription of charms, the writing of petitions, or for recording spells and rituals in your grimoire. While any ballpoint will work in a pinch, finding the time and materials to create your own inks for magical uses can add power and intensity to your Craft. Inks contain ingredients like vinegar and a little bit of alcohol (a preservative); pigments can come from various berries or bark. I personally prefer to use berries when I create inks, because I like how rich pigments can come from them. In my part of New England (in addition to other parts of the US), there grows a plant called pokeweed. The mature plant has vivid fuchsia stems from which eggplant-colored (almost black) berries grow. Though birds can eat the berries unharmed, it is a highly toxic plant for humans. I remember when I first worked with it, I was retching from how badly it smelled. I distinctly remember using paper products to extract the juice from a few sprigs I harvested, because an important thing to know when working with poke berries is that they *will* stain surfaces, your skin, you name it. Pokeweed is a plant used for exorcism and banishing; thus, its berries can be used in an ink for that purpose.

Berries can be foraged in the wild or bought from the grocery store to create your magical ink. The juice from pomegranate arils is ideal for making inks dedicated to workings of the underworldly sort—the dead, ancestors, or offerings to chthonic deities. It is also useful in fertility work. Blackberries make a gorgeous, purple-colored ink, and their properties are of a divinatory nature, as well as for healing and protection. Raspberries make an ink that is perfect for love magic, as well as fertility, luck, and protection. The fruit of the rose, its so-called "hips," are also good for love magic, as well as for working with the Fae, protection, healing, and signing oaths. Rowan berries have protection properties and aid in both divination and psychic development. They are also heavily associated with the Fae. Cherry juice—with its rich, deep red hue—is ideal for inciting lust when used as an ink ingredient. When steeped, bloodroot gives off a rich red shade, which makes a great pigment for use in works of protection and curse-breaking. Though fatally toxic, belladonna berries can be used to craft inks intended for dreaming, spirit flight, baneful magic, and glamouring.

To create your own ink, have with you rubbing alcohol, vinegar, and the berry of your choice. I also recommend using paper goods you can easily dispose of. This is especially useful, not to mention safer, if you are using berries from a baneful plant, as you do *not* want to cross-contaminate them with something you would reuse. You can also add a very tiny amount of another herb that corresponds with what the ink is being made for. Just be mindful not to go overboard; too much could ruin the consistency or color of the ink. Using a disposable paper bowl and plastic spoon, put all of the ingredients together. Mash the berries carefully, and incorporate the alcohol, vinegar, and just a *pinch* of a corresponding herb, if desired. Mix clockwise if this ink is to be used for gain or growth. If it is meant for destruction or decrease, mix counterclockwise until it is fully liquid. Then, using a funnel, pour the newly made ink into a small bottle; ideally, you want to dip a pen into it when the need arises without having to pour it out again. When finished, make sure the bottle is clearly labelled and put in a dark place.

POPPETS

Poppets have long been associated with Witchcraft and are a form of sympathetic magic. They are effigies made in the likeness of a living thing, usually a person or animal, and their use applies the idea of *like affects like*. Simply put, whatever happens to the poppet also happens to the target. Poppets can be made for both baneful and beneficial workings; they are made of such materials as clay, wax, fabric, straw, wood, and more. They also tend to include sympathetic links to the person on whom the spell is being cast—hair clippings, nail parings, photos, and personal belongings. Poppets can be used in such works as binding, cursing, healing, love, and protection.

In crafting a poppet, keeping your focus clear and concise is key. If you are using clay or wax to make your poppet, imagine the person it is meant to represent as you mold and shape it. Try to emulate certain features the person may have. If using wax, it must be warm enough to be malleable, but not dripping hot as if from a candle. You can mix herbs or oils in with the wax or clay, but be sure that there isn't so much as to ruin the material's consistency; otherwise, it will be too difficult to mold. When finished, let the poppet cool and harden. With clay or wax poppets, it's best to use them shortly after you make them.

If using cloth to sew your own poppet, you have a lot of leeway with what you can use to stuff it—batting, cotton balls, beans, herbal mixtures, and so on. Like all your spell work, it is imperative to ensure that the herbs you are using fit your purpose. With cloth poppets, I generally prefer to sew each part of the body individually to the torso, which is the largest part of a poppet. However, you can also cut out body-shaped pieces of fabric (this method is similar to how you'd cut out a gingerbread man). As you sew, imagine this inanimate object coming to life with every stitch. It is being born, symbolically. When you get to stuffing it, leave the top of the head open and stuff each limb and the torso, all the way up to the neck and head of the doll. Stitch it shut, then add features like eyes and a mouth. The beauty of cloth poppets is that once they are made, they can be used at any time after the fact so long as they remain intact.

Straw and wood poppets require a little extra skill to craft properly. You'll need something to bind the material together, as straw and wood tend to be fickle; I recommend twine or glue. Make sure that, like above, your poppet has limbs, a torso, and a head; you may have to get creative with the latter. Due to what they're made of, these kinds of poppets cannot really be stuffed with herbs, but it is a good idea to anoint them with oils.

A commonality with the completion and activation of a poppet—regardless of what it is made of—is baptizing it. By doing this, you are making it officially suitable for magical work. Holy water from a church supplier will do, but even better is a salt and water solution you can make yourself (see Chapter Five, "The Circle of Art and Sacred Spaces," for more). Holding the poppet, pour the water over it entirely and say:

> *Creature of* (material used), *you are baptized by the tides of the West and the salt of the South. You are* (name); *come alive as they are on this earth.*

Then, breathe onto the doll three times and each time, recite:

> *Just as the trees provide us with air, I provide you, (name) with air to breathe. You are now alive. So it is done.*

It is best to perform the baptism when you are in the midst of an actual working—otherwise, the poppet is just a doll and nothing more. If you have long hair, it is a good idea to tie it back so that no rogue strands fall on the poppet. This is especially important when using a poppet in cursing—you do not want a taglock of yourself on the poppet, as it would tie you directly to the outcome. In the same respect, take care not to prick yourself when putting pins into the poppet.

Spell Bags

A handy way to make magic portable, spell bags are found in many practices throughout time and history. In Europe, they usually contained implements that would bring healing or relief for someone suffering from an ailment. In Hoodoo (a type of Southern folk magic), a *mojo* acts similarly and is known as a "prayer in a bag" or *gris-gris* (pronounced *gree-gree*). In this practice, mojo bags can be fixed and fed so that they continue to be effective. This next example is not related to magic in the sense spoken of here, but it is worth mentioning as the relationship between spiritually significant bags and their contents is evident cross-culturally. Many Native American customs include the use of a *medicine bag*, which is worn against the body under the clothes and can contain both personally and spiritually significant items.[71]

From the perspective of Witchcraft, spell bags are used to draw an influence to the one who carries it. They can carry anything relevant to the goal of the work—herbs, tokens, roots, bones, icons, or written charms meant to fulfill a certain purpose. Even the fabric that makes the bag lends its influence—for example, red fabric is ideal for attracting love or good health. A green one is perfect for enhancing fertility or increasing wealth. White fabric is good for attracting blessings or protection, while black is an all-purpose color used when drawing something in. To create a spell bag, you will need to gather implements: an herbal spell mix, suitable oils, a colored pouch with a drawstring, and mini tokens symbolizing your goal. I have included a few select procedures on how to create spell bags for a few different purposes.

PROTECTION DURING SLEEP

Get a small square of fabric that is lavender-colored. If you do not have this color, purple or black is acceptable. Get a lock of your own hair; if you are making this spell bag for someone, get a lock of their hair. Create a mixture of lavender, chamomile, and mullein; the first two herbs are for peaceful sleep,

---

71 Weiser, Kathy. "Medicine Bags or Bundles." *Legends of America,* Sept. 2021, legendsofamerica.com/na-medicinebag/.

while mullein helps protect you during your sleep from unsavory energies or spirits. A small token with an owl on it is a great addition. When done, tie it all together in a bag; kiss the bag as soon as it is closed to seal it. My favorite visualization for this is imagining a sleeping body surrounded by white light that expands from the midpoint of the body outwards, forming a shield. Keep the completed spell bag close to where you sleep.

FOR OBTAINING EMPLOYMENT

Gather the following supplies: a green square of fabric, a whole nutmeg, some money of any denomination (the more it's worth, the better), and symbols of the job you wish to get. For example, if you're looking for a job with a law firm, enclosing a photo of Lady Justice is a good idea. Maybe you're seeking a job in leadership, such as an executive? Add something that reminds you of leadership, especially the kind you want to exude. When ready, close the bag and kiss where you tie it off to seal it. Carry it on the left side of your person when going to job interviews or applying for positions, as the left side corresponds with receptivity. In this sense, you are receiving and obtaining the employment as an end result. Conversely, if you put magical items on your right side, you're projecting or sending out an influence because the right side is projective.

FOR LUCK WITH GAMBLING

Procure a black square of fabric. The idea behind this is drawn from what's known as *poker face*, or a blank expression one wears as to not give away their next move in a card game. If this were of any other color, it would easily catch the attention of those who were to look at it. You will be putting a lucky hand root into the bag, in addition to a bay leaf and a gold coin. You may even opt for a rabbit's foot, a talisman long associated with good luck, or a cat's eye, a gem associated with attainment and enchantment.

As a personal taglock, add nail trimmings from your left hand. Tie the bag together and kiss where the knot lies. Keep it on your left side while playing games of chance.

FOR GOOD LUCK

Get a yellow square of fabric, in addition to a single clover, a dead ladybug or cricket, one acorn, and some heather. Tie it all together, kiss it to seal it, and carry it on your left side to attract good luck.

CORRESPONDENCES

Correspondences can greatly assist a Witch in casting spells and performing rituals. Everything in existence has a correspondence, but we mainly focus on colors, moon phases, moon signs, and timing factors like days of the week. Keep in mind that correspondences may have slight variations due to cultural associations. For example, the color red in China means good luck, while in Italian folk magic, it is employed in protection.

COLORS

Colors can be applied in a bunch of ways when it comes to planning magic—candle colors, fabrics, cords, clothing, inks—the list goes on! That said, if you are set on the idea that you need to own every candle in every color on the visual spectrum, you can stop right there. That's great and all, and you can technically use whatever colors you want, but there are only a handful of common colors used in traditional magic. You don't want to hoard things you may not need; a minimalistic approach is best. The following concise, comprehensive list cuts to the chase and makes choosing the appropriate colors easier:

- **Black:** A color known to be synonymous with Witches, and rightly so—being the complete absence of light, it is extremely powerful. Black is associated with spirit work, conjuration, stability, manifestation, curses, death, endings, and rebirth. It represents feminine, receptive energy; thus, it is a color that *draws in* and absorbs things. Use with caution due to this quality.
- **Red:** A full-bodied color, red is used in works of love, lust, courage, protection, hexes, health, power, and banishing. Red is also used to quicken the results of a working. It's associated with magic that is speedy—or that has a burning, seething quality.
- **White:** This color is popular for its all-purpose nature, perfect for any spell or ritual. It is best known for cleansing, blessing, devotional work, life, birth, truth, learning, consecration, healing, and protection. White represents masculine energy and is projective; in this sense, white is a color that can be used to send something away.
- **Green:** This soothing hue is ideal for workings involving prosperity, fortune, healing, success, fertility, finances, stability, personal growth, development, and especially plant magic. Green can also help if you garden or have a farm that produces food.

DAYS OF THE WEEK, PLANETARY INFLUENCES, AND HOURS

Each day of the week is named after a planetary influence—a fact which, in turn, affects your magic. In English, they are named for the Germanic gods and goddesses, whereas in Romance languages like Italian and French, they are named for their Roman counterparts. Ancient people recognized only seven planets, including the sun and moon, but today, the list of planets in our solar system has grown, and we know the sun and moon are not planets. On the contrary, it is likely that solar and lunar influences were recognized because of their effects on the planet and everything on it—including magic. Read on for some examples of such effects:

- **Sun (*Sunday*):** Leonine magic; success, healing, men, fathers, protection, wealth, courage, glamour, charisma, luck, pride, glory.
- **Moon (*Monday*):** Cancerian magic; intuition, psychic ability, women, mothers, children, weather, divination, emotions, gardening, sleep, dreaming, fertility.
- **Mars (*Tuesday*):** Arian and Scorpion magic; anger, hexing, sex, lust, conflict, revenge, protection, masculinity, destruction, hostility, wrath, discord, victories, health.
- **Mercury (*Wednesday*):** Virgoan and Geminian magic; divination, the mind, healing, communication, networking, speech, writing, magnetism, study.
- **Jupiter (*Thursday*):** Sagittarian and Piscean magic; wealth, money, prosperity, luck, gambling, legal matters, influence, knowledge, expansion, business, honor, gain.
- **Venus (*Friday*):** Libran and Taurean magic; love, friendship, desire, pleasure, luxury, fertility, wealth, harmony, peace, creativity, music, femininity.
- **Saturn (*Saturday*):** Aquarian and Capricornian magic; hexing, cursing, necromancy, binding, endings, death, justice, protection, confusion, limitation, fate, maturity, order.

According to Western occultism, the three outer planets in our solar system (beyond Saturn) are higher octaves of planets that are closer to the Sun. When doing magic with these planetary influences, select the following days to perform them:

- **Uranus (*Wednesday*):** The higher octave of Mercury; Aquarian magic; freedom, innovation, higher consciousness, individuality, intellectualism, originality, intelligence, radicalism, revolution.

- **Neptune (*Friday*):** The higher octave of Venus; Piscean magic; empathy, emotion, truth, visions, spirituality, illusion, imagination, mysticism, addiction, mental health, sobriety.
- **Pluto (*Tuesday*):** The higher octave of Mars; Scorpion magic; rebirth, change, willpower, magnetism, power, chaos, sexuality, regeneration, transformation, necromancy, spirit contact, renewal.

MOON PHASES AND SIGNS

The moon affects the earth in numerous ways, considering it is our closest natural satellite—the tides, our sleeping patterns, our behavior, and yes, magic. Below is a concise explanation of the phases, and how they affect certain workings:

- **New:** This is usually a time of *rest*, but if magic must be done, it should be for new beginnings or setting goals. Just as with the full moon, any endeavor can be taken on when the moon is new.
- **Waxing:** When the moon waxes, it becomes more visible. This is a time for spells of increase, bringing gain, attracting an influence into your life, or drawing something in that you desire.
- **Full:** The most powerful of the phases, any kind of magic can be done during the full moon, especially if it is constructive.
- **Waning:** Spells done to get rid of an influence—to banish, bind, or hex and curse.

The moon enters a new sign every two or three days within the Classical zodiac. Each sign brings a certain influence, as do the planets that were previously mentioned. The Classical zodiac also has body parts associated with it, for the purpose of healing said areas of the body. In medieval Europe, astrology played a role in medicine aside from being a tool in magic or divination. If the moon was in a certain sign, the body part associated with it would be avoided if it needed healing. This rule of thumb was prevalent amongst surgeons of the era. The belief behind this was that the moon controlled bodily fluids, specifically how heavy or light they were. If the moon was, say, in Leo, and a patient needed a heart treatment, he would not be given it until the moon went into the next sign— past the void, of course. As we know, this made no difference because medical treatment was very poor, and people often died regardless. In modern magic, the signs are associated with different influences, but they also stay true to healing the body parts associated with them if need be. When the moon is void, of course (lasting anywhere from minutes to hours), it means it is switching signs; this is *not* a good time to do magic of any kind. It will not work like you want it to, if at all. Void times can be looked up online or in an astrological almanac. See the moon signs below:

- **Aries:** healing of the head; beginnings, the self, swiftness, action, energy, risks
- **Taurus:** healing of the neck, throat; money, wealth, possessions, property, luxury, sensuality, greed
- **Gemini:** healing of the arms, lungs, lymphatic system; communication, writing, inspiration, social engagement, neutrality
- **Cancer:** healing of the breasts, chest; motherhood, marriage, fertility, weather, emotions, sensitivity, children, psychic development, mental health, nostalgia
- **Leo:** healing of the heart, spine; pleasure, creativity, gambling, love, sex, glamour, charisma, men, fathers, authority, projects
- **Virgo:** healing of the digestive system; healing, employment, effort, precision, herbs and plants, fine details, anxiety, change
- **Libra:** healing of the kidneys, lower back; love, partnerships, friendship, beauty, truth, justice, persuasion, contracts

- **Scorpio:** healing of sexual organs and genitals; sex, death, transformation, spirit contact, necromancy, obsession, banishing, chaos, destruction, psychosis
- **Sagittarius:** healing of the hips, thighs; study, learning, travel, freedom, sports, fortune, education, the law, influence, high places
- **Capricorn:** healing of the knees, bones; employment, ambition, karma, time, success, business ventures, long-term goals, order
- **Aquarius:** healing of the shins, ankles; friendship, revolution, psychic awareness, spirituality, science, revelations, surprises
- **Pisces:** healing of feet; spirituality, religion, peace, happiness, the arts, addictions, sleep, substances, deception, illusion, truth, altered states, cleansing

A SPELL WRITING FORMAT

Want to create your very own spells? Fantastic! Things like spells are more powerful when *you* craft them. Here is a helpful format to help:

- **Purpose:** Why are you doing this spell? What do you hope to accomplish? It is imperative that you are as clear and concise as possible in your goals. If you don't know what you want, you cannot expect to get anything.
- **Timing:** When is it? What day of the week, moon phase, and planetary hour are you going by? Timing is of the essence, so plan accordingly. If you are in an emergency situation, there is some flexibility here.
- **Materials:** What tools or implements are you incorporating to help you manifest your desires? Make sure they have to do with the spell you are casting. For example,

you may incorporate a red rose into a love spell you are doing. Using, say, a toy car, would not make sense. In my experience, having knowledge of occult symbolism is a great help when choosing materials and implements to use in spellwork and rituals.

- **Finalize:** What will you say? Will you use gestures? What will you do to raise power? Words have power; your voice is the vehicle that carries them into the aether. Raising power could include a dance, gestures, or chanting.
- **Cast:** Just do it! Take note of any signs during the spell, as well as anything after the fact, including dreams or how fast things are coming to pass. However, do *not* obsess about the outcome—let it work itself out!

SOME SPELLS AND RITUALS

For your own practice of spellwork, I've included a list of spells and rituals. Remember to keep a clear mind and be concise. Speak your will into existence with conviction, and mind the planetary days, moon phases, and other such correspondences.

BANISHING A SPIRIT ATTACHMENT

As mentioned in Chapter Six, "The Old Ones and Other Spirits," under the section "The Departed," spirit attachments are a likely risk when getting in contact with the spirit world. All things in life have risk; we face risk from opening our front door in the morning to driving our cars back home. With spirit work, this is no exception. Just like living people you may encounter on the daily, you may find some spirits are pleasant and some are not; and while this is a part of the balance of life, it's important to protect yourself to mitigate or reduce any risk involved. When working with spirits, I prefer to wear enchanted jewelry pieces with gemstones that have protective properties; they also aid me in connecting to the spirit world. Onyx is a great example of a protective gem, as is amber and many types of agate. One of the hallmark symptoms of a spirit attachment is a sensation that you can feel on any part of the body without a physical etiology. A common theme with this is that it is a fixed point rather than an entire bodily sensation, but it can vary. Other symptoms and signs include feeling drained, hearing voices, feeling so-called "movement" associated with a fixed point on your body, the constant need to look behind you, and a general sense of paranoia. Parasitic attachments—through which you could experience adverse health effects—can be dangerous and must be removed immediately after detection.

This process takes up to two weeks to complete; thus, for the sake of timing, it is best to start on the night of a full moon and have your final night be the dark or new moon. Most of the process, therefore, will occur during the waning moon phase, ideal for banishing and abjuring. It is best to do this before taking a shower. You will need to create an herbal bath of the following plants:

- **Fumitory:** To exorcise and purify; a plant heavily associated with banishing spirits
- **Hyssop:** To banish, purify, and exorcise your body
- **Sage powder:** To purify
- **Basil:** To banish said attachment as well as to keep it away
- **Rosemary:** To purify your body and to protect from future attachments
- **A pinch of salt:** Long associated with banishing and protection; it is one substance considered highly offensive to most spirits

Let the herbs steep in a jar of water for twenty-four hours before you use them. Get rid of any plant matter floating in your mixture. Draw a bath and pour a small amount into the bath water once you have filled the tub enough. Strip down, and step into the bath. As you sit in it, let yourself sink back. Relax, and imagine the properties of the plants working on your physical body to get rid of the attachment. Then, hold your breath, and dunk your head all the way back in the water—this is symbolic of a baptism, a rite of soul purification. As your body is fully submerged, imagine the attachment drowning and weakening in the water imbued with the powers of the plants listed above. If you feel the need to come up for air, do so. Repeat these steps twice more, making it a total of three. Then, recite:

> *By spirit of plants and water in this brew, my*
> *body is pure and my soul is made new.*

Get out of the tub and dry off, letting the water go down the drain. Visualize the attachment going down the drain.

Repeat nightly for two weeks for best results—this is vital in keeping the attachment from coming back. Be mindful also not to surpass the two-week mark, as basil, an ingredient in this bath recipe, can cause topical irritation over long periods of use. After this process is complete, it is wise to ward your home and protect yourself.

To Craft a Witch Bottle

Witch bottles are a form of warding that acts as a decoy and trap for any malicious magic sent your way. The first evidence of Witch bottles comes from seventeenth century England;[72] it is one of a few practices brought over to the New World by settlers.[73] Traditionally, assembling one meant procuring one's urine, hair, and nail parings, as well as needles and red wine if it was suspected that a spell was done on the victim

---

72 "The Mysterious Case of the Witch Bottle." *The Historic England Blog,* 31 Oct. 2016, heritagecalling.com/2016/10/31/the-mysterious-case-of-the-witch-bottle/.

73 Merrifield, Ralph. "Witch Bottles and Magical Jugs." *Folklore,* vol. 66, no. 1, Mar. 1955, pp. 195–207, doi: 10.1080/0015587x.1955.9717455

The Witch bottle was then hidden in an inconspicuous part of the house—buried in the backyard, under the threshold, or, as some discoveries suggest, under the hearth. The latter of these were discovered only after a house was demolished. People went through a lot of trouble to hide their bottles, as they were only effective when they were sealed and intact. So long as this was so, a Witch bottle served as a trap for any malicious magic sent its creator's way. The rationale behind the components is as follows: the maleficia is "impaled" by the nails and needles, "drowned" by the urine or wine, and "sent away" by the rosemary. The biological taglocks serve to connect the bottle to whom it was made for.

A modern twist on this practical spellcrafting method is the following, considering Bellarmine jugs are now pretty rare and expensive. Gather the following implements: a dark-colored bottle or jar (amber or cobalt will suffice), rosemary, sharp objects (pins, needles, nails, broken glass shards, clippings of your hair or nails, and wine. Urine is optional but ideal if you are burying it outside or under your threshold; I don't recommend using urine if you are in an apartment, unable to bury it, and have to hide it in a closet or cupboard. Thorns are also great to use if you have them, but be careful that they don't come from a poisonous plant; handle them carefully. Focus with all of your might on how these implements will work to protect you. Remember what was mentioned above as you put each implement into the jar or bottle:

- **For the sharp objects:** *Creatures of metal and glass, impale all malice and disallow every pass.*
- **For the wine:** *Wine from the grapes of a vine, drown all malice so peace of mind is mine.*
- **If using urine:** *Putrid stench from liquid waste, sterile still to drown the encased.*
- **When adding the rosemary:** *Rosemary, so small but strong, banish all malice and away, string them along.*

- **When adding hair or nail clippings:** *Bottle, I craft you to protect me; thus, I gift you a part of me.*

Seal the bottle tightly. Agitate the bottle, giving it a few shakes and say:

With this bottle I do hide, to trap all malice and evil inside. With all the components placed herein, this entire bottle against evil will win. I command you, bottle of my creation, to trap all malicious harm inside to keep it from harming or affecting me in any way, shape or form. So mote it be.

As it was traditionally done, you can bury this under your threshold or outside near your door. If you are in an apartment or in a shared living environment, hide it in a place where no one can find it and where it will be easy for you to forget about it.

A Spell for Healing

This spell is designed to aid in the recovery process of an illness or injury. Some things to think about before you begin—this spell is not a cure-all, *nor is it* a substitute for conventional medical care. It is an aid in the healing process. When planning this spell, be sure to look at the correspondences provided earlier to see which moon sign is appropriate for the healing of a body part or system. However, if needs are more urgent, go with what feels right in the moment. When working with the moon phases, this spell is best done on a full or new moon. However, if the needs are dire and you have to work with the current phase, use the waxing moon to bring healing to the affected part or person, and the waning moon to banish the illness or injury that befalls the target.

Gather the following implements: a cloth poppet with a taglock of the target sewn into the body (a photograph or lock of hair are good examples), a white ribbon, blessed water, and a red candle. The white ribbon represents your influence over the person's body as healing and restorative, and the red candle is the color of vitality and strength. You may also stuff the body of the poppet with herbs associated with healing, depending on why you're casting this spell. For better precision, you may stuff specific limbs with an herb associated with your purpose. For example, does the target have a fracture or sprain in their right leg or ankle? Stuff the right leg of the poppet with an herb like boneset. Be sure to research the appropriate plants to use if you go with this method. You may perform this spell in a Circle of Art.

Dress the red candle in an all-purpose oil and light it, stating aloud a purpose—you may want to write this out—unique to your situation. What happened to the target? What needs healing? Call upon the Old Ones for this purpose. As you call them forth, feel the exchange of power that comes with their presence: their eyes are your eyes and their hands are your hands, working through you to execute this magic.

Take the poppet and baptize it. While doing so, say:

> *In the Old Ones' name, I baptize you* (name).
> *You are now* (name), *in mind, body, and soul.*

Breathe life into the poppet, exhaling where the mouth of the poppet should be. Then, take out a length of the white ribbon and hold it out. Recite:

> *May this thread be like that of the thread*
> *of life, restoring anything that it touches, an*
> *extension of my intention in action.*

Now, with the ribbon acting as an extension of your healing powers over the target, wrap it over the affected part of the body. Be precise. If the person is suffering from pneumonia, wrap the ribbon over their chest. If the target has a broken leg or arm, wrap the ribbon around that affected part, much like putting a cast on. If the target has had brain surgery and you want to help the recovery process, wrap the ribbon around the head of the poppet. While wrapping it, imagine a white light enveloping the affected part of the target's body, clearing away the affliction and becoming whole and healthy again.

When done, tie the ends of the ribbon and say aloud:

> *In the Old Ones' name, I heal you* (name). *You are free from pain and whole again. Within you, I evoke harmonious synergy between all of your bodily systems, allowing for healing. Bone to bone, blood to blood, flesh to flesh, you are whole again. Like this flame that burns, your vitality and health shall do so once more. So mote it be.*

You may then store the poppet away in a safe space, where you can take it out daily and cuddle it until the person's affliction goes away. By treating the poppet like a baby, you are nurturing it; don't people also do that with the sick or injured? Taking the law of contagion into account, you may also gift the poppet to the person; however, the person needs to know that you're doing this spell for them if you plan to go this route. Once the person's affliction dissipates, dissemble the poppet and burn its contents.

HEALTH SPELL BAG

This spell bag is designed to attract and preserve good health to whomever carries it. When crafting this, make sure you are in a state of good health yourself; because this is meant to draw and preserve, it is important to *be* exactly what it is you are seeking. Health spells are generally effective when done on a waxing or full moon on a Sunday or Tuesday. The sun and Mars are two planetary influences associated with healing and health.

You will need a small red bag with a drawstring, peppermint or eucalyptus oil, snakeskin, the following plant matter: life everlasting, all-heal, peppermint, and orange peels, as well as charms depicting symbols relating to health: caduceus, a snake, fire, heart, or a red cross.

Start by grinding the plant matter; life everlasting is being used for vitality and health, all-heal for balance of bodily systems and functions, peppermint for healing, and orange peels for energy. Add each to your mortar and pestle, saying aloud what they are to do. Once they are ground and mixed, put them in the red bag. The snakeskin represents healing and regeneration. It is being used in this work to draw in the spirit of the snake and its properties. Hold it in your hand and say aloud:

> *Like the serpent sheds its skin and regenerates, so shall all*
> *of my bodily cells regenerate at a normative, healthy rate.*

With each charm listed (whichever you choose), do the same thing: a caduceus incorporates serpentine symbolism because it has two of them intertwined on a winged pole:

> *I am in glowing and radiant health. Like the*
> *serpents on this pole are in perfect synergy, all*
> *of my bodily functions shall be the same.*

Fire is also heavily associated with healing, especially of fevers, which help the immune system fight off viruses and infections. Fire is also a purifier within magic:

> *As fire burns hot and destroys, so shall all manner of*
> *disease, injury, and malady be purified from my body.*

The heart helps us circulate blood and nutrients throughout our veins and arteries. You may even opt to have different organ-shaped symbols within this bag. The red cross symbol is self-explanatory, a symbol of first aid and a certain worldwide healthcare association:

> *Like a doctor's hands can heal and help, so shall
> all current bodily issues resolve quickly.*

Pour a little oil into the full bag. Light some incense that corresponds with health and dangle it over the smoke as you tie it. While tying it, say:

> *Good health is mine, and here to stay; friends within
> this bag, make it go my way. So it is done.*

Then, kiss where you tied the bag and carry it on your person.

TO DRAW FINANCIAL GAIN

This working, designed to draw financial gain, is best performed when the moon is waxing or full. The day of the week ideal for this spell is Thursday; it's most effective during a Jovian hour. As for moon signs, Taurus or Capricorn is the best for working this spell. Procure the following implements: physical currency (coins, bills), one black and one green candle, olive oil, ground bergamot, patchouli incense, offerings that include a fine wine or spirit and a sweet baked good.

You may cast your Circle of Art and call upon the Old Ones. Light the incense and start by anointing the candles with the olive oil, before dressing them in the ground bergamot. This is a plant excellent for use in finances, business, and prosperity. The black candle symbolizes manifestation and earthliness—after all, it is the color of the underworld, said to hold all of the world's riches and resources. The green candle represents growth and financial well-being. Begin by lighting the black candle, putting it behind the green one. Recite:

> *Creature of wax, black as the ground; I summon
> your riches up from the mound. Gold, silver, salt, and
> jewels, with all these treasures, I create accrual.*

Now, close your eyes and imagine a hole in the ground, a faerie hill if you will. Underneath the deep, black soil are treasures that most people would mine and craft into luxurious items. Imagine yourself mining for gold, silver, salt, and gemstones—however, take care to not be greedy in this visualization. Hold out your hands in front of you in a cup shape as you visualize yourself coming back to the surface with the treasures you've found.

Now, light the green candle and say aloud:

> *Creature of wax, green as spring; I summon all*
> *of the fortune you bring. Grow now like a seed*
> *in soil, higher and higher, past the topsoil.*

Picture a seed being dropped into the opening from your last visualization. See it growing slowly, getting taller and stronger. The leaves themselves grow into paper currency, and when the plant is finally mature, imagine that it is leaning down toward you. Its leaves fall off, into your cupped hands. Allow yourself to collect the money it is giving you. Thank the plant for its generosity and open your eyes. Declare aloud three times:

> *I have everything I need. My wallet is full, and my*
> *finances are stable and ever-growing. With every dollar*
> *I spend and invest, I get more back to me. So it is done.*

Make the offerings. The symbolism of having a glass of fine wine with the spirits you're working with is that it is a luxury item. The same goes with the baked good—in times of old, only the wealthy could afford super-sweet, delectable confections. Now that this spell is done, put yourself in the shoes of those who aided you. Take a few bites of the baked good and a few sips of the wine, leaving some for the spirits and Old Ones as thanks. It is done.

TO DRAW A NEW LOVE

Love spells are some of the oldest in the world, but they're also challenging to pull off—and from that, infamous for their consequences. No magic is without personal cost, but this spell here is designed to help the caster draw new love into their life. This is to be performed on a Friday evening, and you may cast it three consecutive Fridays starting with the new moon and ending on a full moon. If you want to do this only once, a full moon is best. Procure the following implements: a red candle (for love and passion), a white candle (for commitment and unity), a black candle (for stability and attracting), incense meant for love workings such as rose, copal, amber, or frangipani, as well as three whole red roses.

Cast a Circle of Art and call upon the Old Ones. Arrange the roses in a triangle, ends to buds and vice versa, in an inverted triangle. At the upper left point, set down the black candle; place the red one at the upper right point. At the point that is facing you, place the white candle down. In the center of the triangle, light your incense and let it burn for a few moments as you gather your thoughts and concentrate.

Begin by lighting the black candle; chant three times:

As the black soil of the earth supports the roots of all,
so it shall also support my quest for love. May the earth
beneath my feet keep stable this new relationship. May my
ideal partner come to me and be made manifest. With this
flame, I set the foundation for a healthy relationship.

Take the time to visualize stability in a relationship. What does this look like for you? Feel free to take your time and reflect on this.

Next, light the red candle and say aloud three times:

As the sun burns brightly in the East, so shall my love life. I ignite
the flame of passion and love and welcome both into my life and
heart. May this new relationship endure forever more.

Like the last step, take some time to reflect on what love and passion mean to you—this could be anything from physical attraction to sharing similar interests in life like careers or hobbies. Imagine that you are attracting a new love that has attributes compatible with yours.

Lastly, light the white candle with the flames of the black and red ones, putting them back in their respective positions. Once this third one is lit, say three times:

> *This flame is formed of union. May it burn to fuel*
> *the commitment between my new love and I, and may*
> *it forge a deep connection between us. As two halves*
> *come together, so shall this be the whole created.*

Finally, declare aloud:

> *Ancient spirits of all these lands, I place my desires into*
> *your hands. This love is mine and here to stay; may all heart-*
> *breakers and players wend away. My love is protected, honest,*
> *and true; darling, I'm here, so come right through! So mote it be.*

Leave offerings and open the space. Leave the ritual setting undisturbed otherwise until the candles burn down. Leave the flowers outdoors as offerings.

GLAMOURING

Glamouring is the art of illusion. It is especially useful in making oneself appear more charismatic and appealing to others, whether for a job interview or a first date. Glamouring is versatile, though, in that it can help downplay your most noticeable features. Perhaps it's one of those days where you do not want people to approach you like they usually do. Want to go unnoticed? Glamouring can help with that. It is an art that not only alters you physically, but also affects your aura and magnetism. The working below serves to *enhance* this. This type of work is best done under lunar influences, so a Monday under a lunar hour is ideal. As for the moon phase, this is best performed when the moon is full and visible in the sky.

You will need a white candle, anointed with an oil and dressed with a mixture of ground lilac petals, white rose petals, and dried datura petals (use caution with the latter of these; datura is very poisonous and has psychotropic effects). You will also need a mirror (one that is able to lay flat on the table facing up as well as set upright), jasmine incense, paper, a pen, and your cauldron.

Find a place that is well-lit by the moon in the sky and set up your implements. Allow the moon beams to bounce off the mirror before you set it upright. Set your dressed candle near the mirror and light it. Recite:

> *Great Mother, your white face shining in the sky, I call upon*
> *your powers so that I may shape and form for all to see.*
> *Lend your silver light for this glamour and unto me.*

Light the candle and take the pen and paper—think about what you wish to achieve with this glamour. Are you going on a date tonight and want to impress the other person? Are you going for a job interview tomorrow and want to increase your chances of being hired? Write down what it takes for you to make these changes. For a first date, for example, you may decide that increasing the prevalence of your attractive qualities will do the trick. For a job interview, you may opt for increased charisma, confidence, and the ability to stand out among all other candidates that applied for that same job. Write down whatever it is, and when done, read it aloud while looking into the mirror. Then take it to the flame of the candle and drop it in the cauldron. As the paper burns and the smoke rises, say aloud:

> *This glamour takes effect now. My desire is*
> *birthed into existence through this vessel.*

Let the candle burn and keep looking in the mirror until you feel comfortable; afterwards, put out the candle. If this is right before an event that evening, groom yourself to perfection. If your event is the next day, light the candle the following day while getting ready.

TO WARD AND SEAL A HOUSE

Aside from Witch bottles or amulets you can hang around a house to protect it, warding and sealing on a monthly basis is another way of keeping your house protected. This process, while simple, takes any amount of time to do, depending on the size of your house or apartment. Before getting started, it is a good idea to burn a cleansing incense to make any unwanted residual energy or spirits leave the space—plants like fumitory or angelica are great for this purpose. Gather the following tools: your dagger and an anointing oil.

First, go around your house and open as many windows as possible. In each and every room, fumigate with the smoke. Declare aloud as you do:

> *May all unwanted or harmful spirits and*
> *influences wend away from this place.*

Repeat for each room. If you live in a house with multiple stories and a basement or cellar, start at the bottommost floor and work your way to the top; the rationale here is to drive all the influences up and out into the aether.

Once this is finished, take your oil and go back down to the bottommost floor of the house. At each window, anoint its top and sill, saying simply:

> *This place is anointed and protected from*
> *any harm that seeks to enter.*

Also do this with any doors that lead to the outside of your house—starting at the top arch of the door and ending down at the threshold—by saying the same thing.

When this process is finished, take your dagger and go to each window and door that leads to the outside of the house. Draw an upright pentagram in the air, starting from the lower left point over the window or door and state aloud:

> *This place is sealed against any harm*
> *or unwanted influences.*

Again, start from the bottommost floor and work your way up. Repeat whenever you feel it is necessary, though once a month while the moon is waning, full, or new will do just fine.

CHAPTER TWELVE

Holidays for Witches

All religions and cultures have their own holidays, as well as reasons for celebrating them. For Witches and other like-minded folks, we have what is commonly known as "the Wheel of the Year." This is a seasonal calendar that is found in many Neopagan circles today, but some of the holidays are quite ancient. There are also variations on these celebrations and what they are named. Witches celebrate these holidays as a way of becoming one with the Earth and her cycles—and to recognize cycles within ourselves with every year we get older. Doing so is also a means of garnering wisdom from the Old Ones and being given gnosis while communing with them. I know that when I do a Sabbat ritual, it is never the same twice. Every year, it is slightly different and holds its own magic and lessons for me to carry into my life.

All Hallows

This holiday is also known as "Samhaín" or, colloquially, "Halloween." Falling on October 31–November 1, this holiday is one of the most (if not *the most*) important of the year. To the Ancient Celts, this celebration marked the new year. To Witches and those of similar paths, All Hallows is a time where those in the spirit world roam the physical plane much more easily, having gained the ability to cross over between planes.

Some like to say the veil is thin, but really, as Witches, we know and recognize that the realms of spirit and form are enmeshed—hence, they are not truly separated. It is an opportune time to honor your dead and ancestors. This ritual helps you do just that, as well as reflect on your own mortality as the earth around you dies, withers, and decays with the coming of winter.

You may decorate an altar space with memorabilia belonging to those who have died—photographs, trinkets, and heirlooms. You may even set down a black altar cloth. Black candles are also to be used in this rite, but keep one for the purpose of lighting it during the ritual. Offerings for this rite include red wine, pomegranate arils, apples, and coinage. One optional piece to have is a skull, either real or fake, to symbolize death and mortality. For this rite, burn an incense like opium, myrrh, or cypress, all of which have long been associated with the dead and the underworld. You also need a sterile medical lancet.

Cast your Circle of Art and call upon the Old Ones to join you. Recite the following words:

Within this circle and in this hour, I call upon
ancestral powers. Blood of blood, bone of bone, I call
you forth and call you home. I invite you here and now,
as I seek communion, guidance, and protection. Hail and
welcome one by one. By my declaration, this rite has begun.

Light the black candle and recite:

May this light guide you here, from the darkness of
the black earth in which your sleeping bones lie.

Using the medical lancet, prick your finger and let a few drops of blood fall on the incense before burning it. Blood is your life force, reminiscent of the tie that binds, and the substance through which thousands of years of your ancestors flows through you. Recite the following after offering the drops of blood:

May this smoke rise up to where souls ascend
and down to where bones are buried.

Wait a few minutes. Close your eyes, and let your mind wander off into a trance state. Feel the spirits of your ancestors making their presences known. You may feel completely surrounded, as though people are standing on the perimeter of your Circle of Art; do not fear, as these are your ancestors. You may even hear them speak or have visions of them. It goes without saying that they could be people you recognize who passed away at some point during your lifetime, or you may not recognize them at all. Feel free to interact with them—you did invite them, after all. Recite aloud once you feel comfortable:

Greetings to all, from many lands and times, known by many names, speaking different tongues, conceivers of many thoughts, ideas, feelings, victories, and failures, I am you. I pay homage to you. I honor you. Thank you for all that has been passed down to me, by you. By blood, bone, and flesh, I walk upon the earth and live my life knowing you are there, and upon my own death, I rejoin you. As much as I am a part of you, so are those after me, born and made flesh on this earth. Thank you, my beloved ancestors, my blood, my family.

Now, turn to the memorabilia in front of you that belonged to the dead. Take each item in hand and reflect on memories you had with the person in question. This is especially useful if you have mementos of those you knew in life. If you have a photo of ancestors from a hundred years ago, you can simply thank them and commune with them through the photograph. Take as much time as you need with this step in the ritual.

Take a beverage and have a sip for yourself before presenting it to the ancestors and the Old Ones as an offering. At this step, also offer food items, like pomegranates, apples, even bread.

Have some for yourself and leave a portion for those whom you invited.

Now, take the coinage and hold it up. In some burial rituals, like that of the Greeks, it was customary to bury the dead with a coin in their mouth to pay the ferryman, who would take the souls of the dead down to Hades.[74] Recite the following to help lost souls find their way back:

> *This coin is an offering to the ferryman, the great psychopomp who carries the deceased from this world into the next. May all lost souls find their way home through your guidance and sense of direction on this night.*

Take a moment of silence before ending the rite:

> *Thank you, Old Ones and ancestors, for communing with me. Though our meeting has ended, know that I am forever with you as you are with me. I wish you peace in your departure from this space; until we meet again.*

Open the circle. Go on as usual with other festivities to celebrate All Hallows. Another customary tradition around this time of year is hosting a *dumb supper*. This is a meal held in total silence in honor of the dead; a place is set out for the deceased, complete with an empty seat. Your menu for the dumb supper can be anything you want, especially if it has significance to your family. For example, you might opt for your mom's Sunday roast with the fixings. Or maybe your great-aunt's clam chowder as an appetizer? I personally like to incorporate a meat dish as a symbol of sacrifice through death—a reminder that death feeds life and will nourish the family through the winter.

---

74 Atsma, Aaron. "CHARON (Kharon) - Ferryman of the Dead, Underworld Daemon of Greek Mythology." Theoi.com, 2017, theoi.com/Khthonios/Kharon. html.

Historically, Samhain was the time of year where the Celtic tribes would sacrifice some of their cattle so that the tribe could survive through the harsh, cold winter months.[75]

To host a dumb supper, have a single white candle at the center of the table. As you are cooking, reflect on what this holiday would mean to our ancient ancestors who did not have the amenities we have today. Set the table and be sure to have hearty portions on each setting. Before beginning, you may say a few words to start the dumb supper, such as:

> *We gather tonight to dine in silence, in honor of the beloved dead. We gather to receive these gifts of nourishment, for it is the sacrifice of death that propagates life and ensures our survival. Old Ones, we thank you. Beloved dead, we invite you here.*

Ring a bell. Afterward, not a sound nor word is to be uttered. Eat and enjoy your meal, reflecting on the dead and the death current. When it seems like everyone in attendance is finished, ring the bell again and say:

> *This supper is concluded, and to you we give thanks for these gifts. May we live to see another year.*

You may also visit the cemetery to leave offerings. These can be at graves where your family members or friends are buried, or if you can identify where more distant ancestors are buried, that is also a great option. The tradition of carving jack-o-lanterns comes from Ireland and seems to symbolize everything from souls in purgatory to a means of protecting the home from unwanted spirits.

---

75 History.com Editors. "Samhain." *HISTORY,* 6 Apr. 2018, history.com/topics/holidays/samhain.

 177

Imbolc

Also known as "Candlemas," this festival is celebrated on or around February 2. The name of this holiday comes from the Gaelic term for *ewe's milk*. It is a festival that heralds the coming of spring as the snow melts away. For those inclined toward the ancient Celtic traditions, this day is associated with the goddess Brighíd, who rules over the hearth, home, and forge. This ritual is designed to honor her.

For this ritual, gather the following: a chalice with milk and bread as offerings, three white candles, your cauldron filled with water, and a floral incense like jasmine or wisteria. You may decorate an altar space with a purple altar cloth or fresh flowers. As for representing the goddess Brighíd, you may opt to have a statuette of her on your altar behind your cauldron of water. Small figurines of farm animals, especially sheep and cows, make great decorations as well.

Cast your Circle of Art and begin the ritual by calling upon the goddess. Light the first candle on the left and say:

> *Great Goddess Brighíd, please come to this rite held*
> *in your honor on this midwinter's night. Brighíd, she*
> *who coaxes the waking seed from the dark, fertile soil;*
> *she who protects all at time of birth; she who is both*
> *maiden and mother of all Ireland; she who is the*
> *red-eared white cow who brings nourishment to all the*
> *people; I ask that you bless this rite and all within it*
> *as you are honored this night. Hail and welcome!*

After a few moments of silence, light the candle to the right and recite:

> *I welcome the warmth and vibrance of Brighíd's*
> *flame to these lands. May we see flowers through*
> *the snows, and colors as tree blossoms grow.*
> *May all see their shadows with the help of her light.*

Take a moment to contemplate and visualize the earth coming back to life after being in the cold, dark winter for a few months. The candle in the middle symbolizes the flame of a sacred well. Bríghíd was associated with these all over the British Isles. Your cauldron with water in it represents the sacred well itself, while the candle represents her sacred fires that were once tended by priestesses. As you light it, recite:

> *Shall the white flame of Leinster enlighten the entire world?*
> *Praise be to Ireland and all of its lands and people!*
> *Blessed Bríghíd, she who is chief of all fine women,*
> *your sacred waters and fires are honored and held here!*
> *May your fires warm and guide my heart and hands.*

Then, give thanks:

> *Many thanks to you, Bríghíd, for your blessings.*
> *As I forever carry your warmth and peace within*
> *me, so shall I teach those I meet of the tidings I bear.*
> *I rejoice in the maiden's presence. And so it is.*

Now it is time for the food and drink offering. Eat and drink a portion of the milk and bread, leaving some for Bríghíd. When you are ready, open the Circle of Art and close the ritual. Let the candles burn in her honor as you continue with other festivities.

BELTANE

Another one of the major festivals of the year is Beltane, celebrated on or around May 1 each year. It is the exact opposite of Samhaín, as this holiday focuses on love, union, and new life starting to come forth. With the latter in mind, it is a time of year where sexuality is greatly honored and respected. It's also around Beltane that the Fae are said to be more present;

in fact, in the British Isles, there was a superstition that babies conceived during this time of year were gifts from the gods and could more easily see and commune with the Fae Folk.[76]

For this ritual—which commemorates the sacred union of the Old Ones and the life that springs forth from said union—decorate your dedicated space with flowers. You may even have a miniature maypole set up with ribbons. Choose a floral incense, such as lilac, rose, plumeria, or another sweet scent; you may also opt for an earthy scent like patchouli. Have two green candles on either side of a white candle, as well as your dagger and a chalice with wine. Have bread or another baked good as an offering ready.

Cast your Circle of Art and call upon the Old Ones. Open the ritual by lighting the incense and reciting:

> *I call upon the ancients, on this day and in this hour.*
> *I call forth the Flower Maiden and the Green Horned*
> *God to this space in celebration of your union as all*
> *of nature and the world rejoices. Hail and welcome!*

Take a few moments and light the candle to the left, representing the feminine, the flower bride. Say aloud:

> *I light this flame to evoke the presence of the mother, she*
> *who is the bride covered in flowers, draped in white, the*
> *Queen of the Fae and of the Sabbat. Your presence is*
> *celebrated, welcomed, and appreciated on this day.*

Then, light the candle to the right, representing the masculine, the horned father:

---

76 Wigington, Patti. "Legends and Lore of the Beltane Season, the Spring May Day Celebration." *Learn Religions*, 14 Feb. 2018, learnreligions.com/legends-and-lore-of-beltane-2561642.

I light this flame to evoke the presence of the father, he who is King of all wild places and creatures, the leaf-masked man in the foliage, the master of the Sabbat. Your presence is celebrated, welcomed, and appreciated on this day.

Next, light the white candle in the center by taking the two green ones and lighting the white wick with those flames. After it is lit, recite:

From your union shall new life spring forth. As the winds blow from all directions, and all life covers the earth, I celebrate unity and love on this day. Shall this flame of holy union be that which drives all creative forces during this merry May season.

Now it is time to symbolically perform *heiros gamos,* or "sacred union." In your left hand, take the chalice, and in your right, take the dagger. Lower the dagger's blade into the chalice of wine and say aloud as you do:

Male is to female, as chalice is to blade, as sun is to moon and sky is to earth, as above so below, as within so without. All aspects of the realms of spirit and form come together into union.

Drink some of the wine and eat some of the bread. Leave some of each as an offering to the Old Ones before closing the rite and opening your Circle of Art. For Beltane, there are other ways to celebrate as well—one famous example of a tradition during this time of year is a maypole dance and the crowning of the May Queen. Indulging in sexuality is also a good way to celebrate this holiday, in addition to feasting and making crafts involving flowers.

LUGHNASADH

Also known as Lammas, this is celebrated on or around August 1, and commemorates the first harvest of the season. Late summer was (and still is, depending on where you live) the time of year where oats, grains, and barley could be harvested to make bread and beer. It is also when the earth around us starts to feel some semblance of the dark half of the year. The name of this festival comes from one of the Celtic sun gods, Lugh. For this ritual, recommended decorations for your altar space include a golden-colored tablecloth and beeswax tapers. You may also have a decorative cinnamon broom and wheat straws sticking out of a vase. You will need the following for the actual ritual: a white candle, bread (store-bought or baked), and beer.

Cast your Circle of Art and call upon the Old Ones. Begin by reciting:

It is now Lughnasadh, the first harvest of the year.
On this day, I reap the first rewards of my labor and
relish in the plenty that it brings. To the Old Ones, I offer
part as thanks, in gratitude for the lessons taught to me.

Light the white candle. While closing your eyes, imagine a field of gold before you. All of the year's crop is prime and ready for harvesting, but you admire the result of the year's work beforehand. Recite:

I thank the earth for her bounty and plenty. I have little need for
food, for I am plentiful and always satisfied. Lady of the Golden
Harvest, nourish us all forevermore. In the cold dark winters,
nourish us all. In the storms and in the rain, nourish us all.

Look at the flame, and after a few deep breaths, acknowledge the hunter aspect of the Horned One:

*Old Lord of the Dance, King of the Wild Hunt, with this
flame I give thanks for leading me into the deeper mysteries of
my heart. I give thanks for your sacrifice, and for teaching us
how to survive and thrive. With this flame and in this rite,
I open my heart to the mysteries of life, death, and rebirth.
By hoof and horn, all that dies shall be reborn. By corn
and grain, all that falls shall rise again. So mote it be.*

Now it is time to share the symbolic meal and drink with the
Old Ones to celebrate the abundance of the harvest season.
Hold the bread dish in your right hand and your cup of beer in
the left, then say aloud:

*The circle of life is contained here within this food
and drink. Birth, death, and birth again, over and
over, the cycle of life goes on. I give thanks.*

Eat part of the bread and drink half of the beer, leaving the rest
as an offering for the Old Ones. Take as much time as you need
at this point of the rite to reflect on what you have achieved in
the past year; it doesn't have to literally be related to harvesting
grains. It can be anything—did you start a new job? Did you
have some other milestones happen, like getting married or
having a baby? Did you move into a new house? Did you start
a new business, or start a creative project that you are very
proud of? Consider all these things, and how you feel about them.
Let yourself revel in the rewards of your labor, and end the rite
when you are ready by declaring:

*I thank you, Old Ones; from dawn to dusk, you keep us
safe and allow us the resources to find and carve our ways
on this earth. As you go forth from this space, I hold you
dear and am forever open to the lessons and gifts you bring
to us all. To the sun, I bid farewell until the dark of winter
brings you back again in the flames of enlightenment.*

Creating corn dollies out of corn husks is also a way to celebrate this festival; if you have children, it is a fun way to get them involved with the celebrations. Creating a corn god out of bread is also not unheard of—this is a special bread in the shape of a human figure. Going back to this holiday's namesake, Lugh is colloquially known as "John Barleycorn" in England; he is the very essence of the grain that makes the bread. Thus, this corn god bread doll is symbolically sacrificed and eaten, representing the immortality found in the circle of life—John Barleycorn had to die to make bread but is reborn in the seeds of the crop for next year.

ℱAREWELL: 𝒜 𝒯IMELESS 𝒜RT

Now that you've made it to the end of this book, I sincerely hope you have learned something new—perhaps two? Three? Or maybe this is one of those books that, years later, in its entirety, will be considered one that greatly influenced your personal Craft? Either way, let this book not be the last you read on the Craft. One of the most important things to growing and learning within a particular subject is expanding your horizons. Yet, one thing is for certain—you cannot become a Witch overnight or just because a social media influencer said anyone can. You may be born with the predisposition, but it takes years of dedication, study, and commitment to developing not only your skills but your relationship with the realm of spirit.

Books are fantastic in and of themselves; for me, at least, they're a go-to when it comes to learning. That said, since the inception of the World Wide Web, browsing has become king in the world of research. Truly learning the Craft comes from experiences that books or the Internet will not teach you. Go outside—don't just notice the season and weather; take in *everything* around you, including that. Is it raining with distant thunder and lightning brewing in the sky? Be in awe of its natural wonder. Do not tremble in fear. Is it hot and humid? It may feel unpleasant, but remember that in this weather, life of all shapes and sizes can thrive. Is it bone-biting cold with the trees having long since shed their leaves? Keep warm, of course, but remember that the cold preserves all it touches—those trees are still standing strong, and the ground beneath you may seem barren, but it holds the potential and secrets of Nature herself. Most (if not all) of these secrets are revealed in time, as you're able to handle them.

The concept of time often takes a backseat in our lives— we do not consciously think about it. That is, until we have a birthday pass by, and we're made a year older. A relative or friend you have known for a long time may pass away, causing you to reflect on all of the years you spent with that person, and all of the memories you shared. You may think of time passing as a curse; as an adult, you may find the latest trends, music styles, or fads cringe-worthy and long for better days from when you were younger. The only way through is forward, but when you listen to music you once enjoyed as a child, engage in activities you once found enjoyable, or even wear that old pair of jeans that still fit you from high school, it is like you are going back. Well, if only in mind. Time is of the essence, and within the Craft, it holds true as much as it does in a mundane sense. That is because within a circle, there's a place between space and time, a meeting place for the realms of spirit and form to fully connect. In that circle, we reweave the fabric of destiny to shape the reality of our future. When it catches up to you, you can see every string you pulled falling back into place. Time also plays a role in divination. I'd like to think of this as a form of perceiving time through different angles: the past, present, and future. In the near or distant past, something had to have happened to lead you to where you are now—reading this book on your couch, bed, or even on a park bench. In the present, things are happening to lead up to your future. What is here now, we can change with the resources we have or are given.

The Old Craft is truly a timeless art—as a practitioner of said art, you are able to shape and transform reality, unlike most other people. The Old Craft is not only timeless, but it tran- scends such human constructs as politics, social class, language, culture—the list goes on. It is paradoxical to think that the Old Craft functions within and without the known structure and flow of time. No matter how many years I've practiced it, it never ceases to amaze me, nor has it ceased to teach me every-thing I am ready to know at a given point.

The Sun may rise and set, the Moon may show its phases each day of the month, the leaves of a tree may appear and disap-pear with the changing of the seasons. The spirits of the land will always be present, and they too are timeless. As for you? You are timeless, as is your own essence and spirit. The progression of time may cause you to physically break down and wither until there is nothing left but your bones at their final resting place in the ground. Even then, you are timeless and infinite. If you feel the spark inside you even after reading, let it become a fire that enlightens and fulfills you. Let it be your drive. Remember: a fire needs to be controlled, lest it consume everything around it—this control will be your greatest strength.

Best of luck.

BIBLIOGRAPHY

Amaranthus. *Feasting from the Black Cauldron: Teachings from a Witches' Clan.* Pendraig Publishing, 2018.

"Atropine Injection." Cleveland Clinic, my.clevelandclinic.org/health/drugs/19824-atropine-injection.

History.com Editors. "Samhain." *HISTORY,* 6 Apr. 2018, history.com/topics/holidays/samhain.

Berkshire Law Library. "Witchcraft Law up to the Salem Witchcraft Trials of 1692." Mass.gov, 31 Oct. 2017, mass.gov/news/witchcraft-law-up-to-the-salem-witchcraft-trials-of-1692.

Blacker, Carmen. *The Catalpa Bow: A Study of Shamanistic Practices in Japan.* Routledge, 2004.

Bogdan, Henrik. "The Influence of Aleister Crowley on Gerald Gardner and the Early Witchcraft Movement." Brill, 1 Jan. 2009.

Cal, Frances. "Persian and Indian Playing Cards." *Eastern Art at the Ashmolean Museum,* 2 Nov. 2017, blogs.ashmolean.org/easternart/2017/11/02/persian-and-indian-playing-cards/.

Cameron, Malcolm Laurence. *Anglo-Saxon Medicine.* Cambridge University Press, 1993.

Cartwright, Mark. "Gundestrup Cauldron." *World History Encyclopedia,* 15 Feb. 2021, worldhistory.org/Gundestrup_Cauldron/.

Charles, R H. *The Book of Enoch*. Dover Publications, 2007.

Chauran, Alexandra. "Understanding Elementals." Llewellyn Worldwide, 11 Nov. 2013, llewellyn.com/journal/article/2399.

"Complaint of Susannah Trimmings, of Little Harbour, Pascataqua." Witchcraft in New Hampshire - 1656, 18 Apr. 1656, n6jv.com/tena/witch.htm.

Conway, David. *Magic: An Occult Primer: 50 Year Anniversary Edition*. The Witches' Almanac, 2022.

Coleman, Martin. *Communing with the Spirits: The Magical Practice of Necromancy Simply and Lucidly Explained, with Full Instructions for the Practice*. Red Wheel/Weiser, 1998.

Cooke, Justin. "Datura: Risks, Experience & Trip Reports." *Tripsitter*, 20 Mar. 2021, tripsitter.com/datura/.

"Cross-Cultural Trade and Cultural Exchange during the Crusades." *The Sultan and the Saint*, 2019, sultanandthesaintfilm.com/education/cross-cultural-trade-cultural-exchange-crusades/.

"Crowley's Pyramid of Power." *Occult Search Engine, Archive and Book of Shadows for Witchcraft, Paganism, Spells, Magick, Rituals, Wicca, Satanism, Tarot, Psychics, Ouija, Divination and Other Esoteric Topics*. Online.

Dashú, Max. "Wu: Ancient Female Shamans of Ancient China." *Suppressed Histories*, 2011, suppressedhistories.net/articles2/WuFSAC.pdf.

Davenport, John. "The Witches of Huntingdon, Their Examinations and Confessions; Exactly Taken by His Majesties Justices of Peace for that County." Early English Books, 1646, quod.lib.umich.edu/cgi/t/text/text-idx?c=eebo2;idno=A81978.0001.001.

David, Marie Nicole V., and Mrin Shetty. "Digoxin." National Library of Medicine, 19 Jan. 2023, ncbi.nlm.nih.gov/books/NBK556025/.

Davies, Melissa. "Isobel Gowdie - Witch of Auldearn." Discover the Highlands and Islands of Scotland, discoverhighlandsandislands.scot/en/story/isobel-gowdie-witch-of-auldearn.

Delistraty, Cody. "The Surprising Historical Significance of Fortune-Telling." *JSTOR Daily*, 26 Oct. 2016, daily.jstor.org/surprising-historical-significance-fortune-telling/.

della Porta, Giambattista. *Natural Magick by John Baptista Porta, a Neapolitane.* Legare Street Press, 2021.

Desborough, Michael J. R., and David M. Keeling. "The Aspirin Story - from Willow to Wonder Drug." *British Journal of Haematology*, vol. 177, no. 5, 20 Jan. 2017, pp. 674–683, doi: 10.1111/bjh.14520

Descent of Inanna. University of North Carolina Wilmington, 2 Apr. 2009, people.uncw.edu/deagona/myth/descent%20of%20inanna.pdf.

Dow, Steve. "Goodwife Walford the Witch." *My New England Ancestors*, Nov. 2018, newenglandancestors.weebly.com/blog/goodwife-walford-the-witch.

"Elizabeth I (R.1558-1603)." The Royal Family, 3 Aug. 2018, royal.uk/elizabeth-i.

"Elves in Norse Mythology." *Nordic Culture*, 24 Sept. 2020, skjalden.com/elves/.

"Eunice 'Goody' Cole." Hampton Historical Society, 2011, hamptonhistoricalsociety.org/gcole.htm.

"Eunice Cole, the Witch of Hampton Who Could Not Be Stopped." *New England Historical Society*, 1 Oct. 2019, newenglandhistoricalsociety.com/eunice-cole-the-witch-of-hampton-who-could-not-be-stopped/.

Frisvold, Nicholaj and Katy de Mattos. *The Canticles of Lilith.* Troy Books, 2022.

Gary, Gemma. *Traditional Witchcraft: A Cornish Book of Ways.* Troy Books, 2008.

Genesis 4. *The Holy Bible: New International Version.* Zondervan, 1984.

Graves, Robert, and Grevel Lindop. *The White Goddess: A Historical Grammar of Poetic Myth.* Farrar, Straus, and Giroux, 2013.

Greco, Karen. "The Witches of Providence." *Providence Monthly,* 30 Sept. 2022, providenceonline.com/stories/the-witches-of-providence,99049#.

Green, W. C., translator. "Egil's Saga." Icelandic Saga Database, 1893, sagadb.org/egils_saga.en

Grimassi, Raven. *Grimoire of the Thorn-Blooded Witch: Mastering the Five Arts of Old World Witchery.* Weiser Books, 2014.

Gonzalez-Wippler, Migene. *The Complete Book of Spells, Ceremonies, and Magic.* Llewellyn Worldwide, 1978.

Harker, Joe. "'World's Scariest Drug' Has Been Used by Organised Crime Gangs." UNILAD, 22 Aug. 2022, unilad.com/news/worlds-scariest-drug-crime-gangs-20220822.

Harrison, Dick and Kristina Svensson. *Vikingaliv.* Natur och kultur, 2007.

Heiduk, Matthias, Klaus Herbers, Hans-Christian Lehner, Walter de Gruyter, eds. *Prognostication in the Medieval World: A Handbook.* De Gruyter, 2020.

History.com Editors. "Samhain." HISTORY Channel, 6 Apr. 2018, history.com/topics/holidays/samhain.

"How Long Do Dreams Last?" Healthline, 10 Feb. 2020, healthline.com/health/how-long-do-dreams-last#how-long-dreams-last.

Howard, Michael. *Children of Cain.* Three Hands Press, 2019.

The Book of Fallen Angels. Capall Bann, 2004.

Horne, Roger J. *Folk Witchcraft: A Guide to Lore, Land, & the Familiar Spirit for the Solitary Practitioner.* Moon Over the Mountain Press, 2021.

Huson, Paul. *Mastering Witchcraft.* G.P. Putnams, 1970.

"Information about Kipper Cards." The Fortune Tellers Society, 1 Dec. 2017, thefortunetellerssociety.com/information-about-kipper-cards/.

Isidora. "Isis & the Magic of Myrrh." *Isiopolis,* 20 July 2013, isiopolis.com/2013/07/20/isis-the-magic-of-myrrh/.

Jackson, Nigel and Michael Howard. *The Pillars of Tubal Cain.* Capall Ban, 2001.

Johnson, Caleb. "Crime and Punishment in Plymouth Colony." MayflowerHistory.com, 2014, mayflowerhistory.com/crime.

Karlsen, Carol F. *The Devil in the Shape of a Woman: Witchcraft in Colonial New England.* W.W. Norton and Company, 1998.

Landrigan, Leslie. "The Candlemas Massacre and the Salem Witch Trials." New England Historical Society, 1 Mar. 2017, newenglandhistoricalsociety.com/candlemas-massacre-salem-witch-trials/.

Leland, Charles G. *Aradia: Gospel of the Witches.* 1899.

Lévi, Éliphas, and Arthur Edward Waite, translator. *Transcendental Magic: Its Doctrine and Ritual.* Martino Fine Books, 2011.

Love, Dane. *Legendary Ayrshire: Custom, Folklore, Tradition.* Carn Publishing Limited, 2009.

Magnus, Grayson. *Authentic Witchcraft: A Historical Tradition Revealed.* N.p.: CreateSpace, 2013. Print.

McKay, Andrew. "Viking Runes: The Historic Writing Systems of Northern Europe." *Life in Norway,* 21 Aug. 2020, lifein-norway.net/viking-runes/.

Merrifield, Ralph. "Witch Bottles and Magical Jugs." *Folklore*, vol. 66, no. 1, Mar. 1955, pp. 195–207, doi: 10.1080/0015587x.1955.9717455

Muise, Peter. *Witches and Warlocks of Massachusetts: Legends, Victims, and Sinister Spellcasters.* Globe Pequot, 2021.

Murray, Margaret Alice. *The Witch-Cult in Western Europe.* 1921.

Newman, Tim. "How Do Penicillins Work?" Medical-NewsToday, 30 July 2018, medicalnewstoday.com/articles/216798#history.

Notestein, Wallace. *A History of Witchcraft in England from 1558 to 1718.* Gutenberg, 2010.

Oldridge, Darren. "Fairies and the Devil in Early Modern England." *The Seventeenth Century*, vol. 31, no. 1, Jan. 2016, pp. 1–15. doi: 10.1080/0268117X.2016.1147977

"Opium Poppy." Drug Enforcement Administration Museum, museum.dea.gov/exhibits/online-exhibits/cannabis-coca-and-poppy-natures-addictive-plants/opium-poppy#:~:text=Morphine%3A%20In%201803%2C%20morphine%2C.

Pagliuco, Chris. "Connecticut's Witch Trials." Wethersfield Historical Society, 2007, www.wethersfieldhistory.org/articles/connecticuts-witch-trials/.

Parlett, David. "Tarot | Playing Card." *Encyclopedia Britannica*, 7 Apr. 2009, britannica.com/topic/tarot.

Peterson, Joseph H. *Grimorium Verum: A Handbook of Black Magic.* Scotts Valley, CA: CreateSpace, 2007. Print.

Pahnke, Janis. "The Strange Case of Elizabeth Knapp", The Bigelow Society, July 1997. bigelowsociety.com/elizabeth_knapp.html

R. Whalen. "Sorginak and the Basque Witch Trials." *Basque at the University of Illinois at Urbana-Champaign,* 21

Feb. 2015, basqueuiuc.wordpress.com/2015/02/21/ sorginak-and-the-basque-witch-trials/.

Revak, James W. "Biography of Etteilla / Great Tarotists of the Past." Villarevak.org, 2001, villarevak.org/bio/ etteilla_1.html.

Rogak, Lisa. *Stones and Bones of New England.* Rowman & Little-field, 2016.

"Samuel Scripture of Groton." Rjohara.net, rjohara.net/gen/ scripture/.

Sedgwick, Icy. "Hawthorn Folklore: Fairies and the May Day Tree." Icy Sedgwick, 28 Nov. 2020, icysedgwick.com/ hawthorn-folklore/.

Sirach. *The Alphabet of Ben Sira.* Valmadonna Trust Library, 1997.

Schulke, Daniel A. *Veneficium: Magic, Witchcraft and the Poison Path.* Three Hands Press, 2018.

Viridarium Umbris. Xoanon Publishing, 2005.

"SWP No. 063: Sarah Good Executed July 19, 1692." Salem Witch Trials Documentary Archive, salem.lib.virginia.edu/ n63.html.

--. "Important Persons in the Salem Court Records." 2002, https://salem.lib.virginia.edu/people/.

Thayer, Bill. "Pliny the Elder: the Natural History." penelope. uchicago.edu/thayer/e/roman/texts/pliny_the_elder/ home.html.

The Atwell Family. "Sarah Towne of Salem, Massachusetts, Part 2: The Accusers and Accused." *Tree of Many Leaves,* 30 May 2019, treeofmanyleaves.com/treeofmanyl-eaves/2019/4/11/sarah-towne-of-salem-massachusetts-part-2-the-accusers-and-accused.

"The Mabinogion: Math the Son of Mathonwy." Sacred-Texts.com, sacred-texts.com/neu/celt/mab/mab26.htm.

"The Mysterious Case of the Witch Bottle." *The Historic England Blog*, 31 Oct. 2016, heritagecalling.com/2016/10/31/the-mysterious-case-of-the-witch-bottle/.

The Mythcrafts Team. "The Fox as Familiar: Japanese Witchcraft." Myth Crafts, 9 Aug. 2018, mythcrafts.com/2018/08/09/the-fox-as-familiar-japanese-witchcraft/.

Tucker, Abigail. "The Great New England Vampire Panic." Smithsonian Magazine, Oct. 2012, smithsonianmag.com/history/the-great-new-england-vampire-panic-36482878/.

Wallace, Lorna. "10 Royals Who Dabbled in the Occult." *Listverse*, 17 Nov. 2022, listverse.com/2022/11/17/10-royals-who-dabbled-in-the-occult/.

Walsh, Sarah Nell. "Courtroom Examination of Bridget Bishop." University of Virginia, Sept. 2001, salem.lib.virginia.edu/people/bishop_court.html.

Weiser, Kathy. "Medicine Bags or Bundles." Legends of America, Sept. 2021, legendsofamerica.com/na-medicinebag/.

Whalen, R. "Sorginak and the Basque Witch Trials." Basque at the University of Illinois at Urbana-Champaign, 21 Feb. 2015, basqueuiuc.wordpress.com/2015/02/21/sorginak-and-the-basque-witch-trials/.

"What Are Wights?" Fyrnsidu, 17 Aug. 2021, fyrnsidu.faith/wights/.

Wigington, Patti. "Legends and Lore of the Beltane Season, the Spring May Day Celebration." *Learn Religions*, 14 Feb. 2018, learnreligions.com/legends-and-lore-of-beltane-2561642.